GOOD 2 GO

The author of the Flipping Numbers series

PRESENTS

A Hustler's Dream

Ernest Morris

Good2Go Publishing

A Hustler's Dream

Written by Ernest Morris
Cover Design: Davida Baldwin
Typesetter: Mychea
ISBN: 978-1-943686-55-1

Copyright ©2016 Good2Go Publishing
Published 2016 by Good2Go Publishing
7311 W. Glass Lane • Laveen, AZ 85339
www.good2gopublishing.com
https://twitter.com/good2gobooks
G2G@good2gopublishing.com
www.facebook.com/good2gopublishing
www.instagram.com/good2gopublishing

Being on top always comes at a price. For these two friends, that spot may cost them their lives. **Donte** (aka **Worlds**), whose name is heavy on the streets of Chester, wants to come home, make enough money to turn legit, and get out of the game. Not knowing what he's getting into, he has his friend Fredd (a dude from Philly he met in prison) set up a business deal just in case he's released.

Because **Fredd** is unable to leave his conniving, scheming habits behind him, he takes something from the wrong people. This starts up a beef that places Worlds right in the midst of an all-out war that he never saw coming.

Dominique is an ambitious twenty-five-year-old good girl, who falls in love with a street nigga. She has a sassy, smart mouth and a stubborn attitude to go with it. All she wants is for Donte to marry her and stop messing around. Fed up with the cheating and lies, she tries to leave him, but will her love for him bring her back?

This book is another bestseller filled with murder, drugs, sex, lies, and so much more. It will keep you on the edge of your seat.

Every **Hustler's Dream** is to make it out of the hood rich, and live. Will these friends live that dream, or will they die trying? Loyalty is everything. Or is it?

Acknowledgements

First and foremost, I have to give thanks to the Man above for continuing to keep me safe. Whether it was in these chaotic streets of Philly or behind those walls, you have always kept an angel in my presence.

I want to once again thank everyone at **Good2Go Publishing** for supporting and believing in me. I never could have done this without you. You have devoted a lot of time, trust, and money in me to keep writing novels that will keep the fans wanting more. I hope that it continues to pay off.

To all my fans and followers, thank you for staying true to me and keeping me leveled. You are what inspires me to do what I do, and I truly appreciate you.

I want to give a shout-out to all my Passyunk family. They took the buildings, but left the name, memories, and love.

Last but not least, to all my family and friends, thank you for having my back. I love y'all, and once again, let's get this money.

Dedications

Once again, I would like to dedicate this book to my mother and sister (RIP), who are up in heaven smiling down on me for my success. Thank you for keeping me grounded and focused. Whenever my mind wandered off, y'all brought me back to where I needed to be. Until I get to see you again, a piece of my heart will forever be broken.

Chubb and Walid, look at your brother. I am doing this for all of us. Every time my pen touches the paper, it is hopefully to one day get us out of the struggle. It is a long journey, and I cannot do it by myself; but together, we can conquer anything. I love y'all, and keep ya heads up.

To my kids, my life is nothing without you. There are always going to be obstacles that will get in your way, but never give up. Always fight for what you believe, and eventually you will win. Whatever you want to be in life, go for it, and turn those dreams into reality.

To Omar, Piper (Pike), and Knowledge (South Philly), that door is about to open up to those prison walls. It just takes patience and hope. Each one of you has inspired me in different ways. I want you to know that I will never forget about you. Stay strong in there, and I will see you on the other side when we hit those Passyunk reunions up.

To everyone at the Cheesecake Factory: A.J., Katz, John, Shelly, Arnold, Kayla, Marcus, Jade, Will, Evani, Lope, Dom, Rhonda, Christina, Janette, Morgan, Tia, Jalisa, Ty, Bill, London, Melissa, Toya, Stacks, Dawn, Sarah, Torey, Edward, Nestor, Nancy (both), Mia, and everyone else who I missed, you know who you are, thanks for letting me be a part of the winning team.

Prologue

"No one can stop us now, bro. The competition is no longer a problem, and everybody knows that we run the city," Fredd stated, sipping a glass of E&J.

Worlds sat on the ottoman, puffing on some loud as he thought about all the treacherous things he and his crew had done to take over the cities of Chester and Philadelphia. They had committed murder after murder, until there was no one left standing but them. "Yeah, but where does that leave us now? We lost a lot of good soldiers in the process," he replied.

"Come on, ock! They knew what they were getting into when they decided to bang with us. It could have easily been one of us lying in the dirt right now. They gave their lives for us, and for that, we will make sure their families are taken care of,"

Fredd spat, walking back and forth across the balcony. "Besides, I know the infamous Donte is not getting soft on me."

"Nigga, I told you about calling me by my government. I'm not getting soft. I'm just looking at the big picture. Yeah, we control the drug trade, but I want more. I want to open up some businesses to cover up our illegal endeavors," Worlds said as the two men looked out at the peaceful city.

"What do you have in mind?"

"I was thinking about investing in a couple of things. Look at what's going on in Atlantic City with the casinos. How about we look into that or maybe some apartment complexes?" Worlds asked.

"That sounds good and all, but how the hell are we going to get into that when neither one of us has any business experience? We both dropped out of high school and have criminal records."

"I can get Dom to get a business license, so let me worry about that. Let's get out of here and go check on this money. Besides, I have to pick up my kids in a few. I'm taking them to Chuck E Cheese's since I haven't seen them in a month because of all the beef we were in," Worlds stated as the two men headed out of the penthouse.

As they stepped off the elevator and headed toward the garage, where their cars were located, they never saw the three black SUVs creeping up on them.

* * *

"Damn! What's taking your dad so long to get here? I've called him four times already, and he hasn't even answered once," Amanda said to little Payton.

She just sat there playing with her Barbie doll, not even paying attention to her mom. Katie walked in with two glasses of Moet and passed one to her sister.

"You know how he is. The only thing he ever been on time for was collecting money from his raggedy-ass workers. Other than that, he's late as hell!" she said. The two of them burst out laughing as they downed their drinks before setting the empty glasses on the table. Amanda huffed and then leaned her head back on the couch.

"I have to work tonight, so he better hurry up and get here, or you will have to watch the kids for me."

"I have a date tonight, Manda. I told you about that the other day. I've been standing bull up for a minute now. I finally told him that we can chill tonight," Katie replied.

"He'll be here to get them before your friend comes. Don't act like that," Amanda stated as she playfully punched her sister in the arm.

Before she could respond, they heard the baby crying in the other room. Amanda got up and went to get Donnie Jr., and Katie threw a pillow at her and then grabbed the glasses to refill them.

When Amanda looked at her son, he was the spitting image of Worlds. He couldn't deny him if he tried. She thought back to the day when Worlds first came into her parents' pizza shop for a slice. It only took one date for him to win her over. She had never been with a black guy before, so curiosity got the best of her, and once they had sex the first time, she was addicted.

They spent every available moment together that they could. Worlds showed her a lot of attention in the beginning, but once he started wreaking havoc from city to city, he stopped being around her so much. He didn't want her to get caught up in the life that he kept a secret from her. One day she was driving down the street because she wanted to surprise him with a tattoo that she just got, when she heard rapid gunfire. She saw some guy do a flip in the air and land in the middle of the street, right in front of her car. All of a sudden, someone walked up to the guy lying there, and emptied his clip into him, causing his body to jerk.

She couldn't believe her eyes when she saw the man she was in love with standing with the smoking gun. Their eyes met as he ran up to the passenger side of her car. She unlocked the door as Worlds jumped in. No words were spoken as she hit the gas, getting him out of there and away from the crime scene. She never even mentioned what she saw that day. Worlds realized he had a girl in his corner who was down for whatever, which made him like her even more. Now they were engaged to get married and had two beautiful children together. Amanda knew that he would do anything to protect his family, and she would be by his side no matter what.

"Amanda! Manda!" Katie yelled, snapping her out of her thoughts.

Amanda looked up at her sister and smiled.

"Don't he look just like his ugly-ass dad, but more handsome?" Amanda said, with a smile on her face.

"You're stupid, girl! I just talked to my date and told him that I may be running late, so go ahead and get ready for work. I'll watch the kids until he comes," she told her. She picked up little Donnie and gave him a bunch of kisses on his cheeks, causing him to chuckle.

"Thanks, Sis! I owe you big for this one," she stated as she headed for her room to get dressed.

"You sure do, and I will be collecting for it, too," Katie replied as she took Donte into the other room with her.

When Amanda left for work, she tried calling Worlds again, but had the same results. It wasn't like him not to answer her calls. She couldn't shake the feeling that something was wrong. If she only knew that the feeling she was having would soon be a reality.

Welcome to A Hustler's Dream

A Hustler's Dream

Ernest Morris

One

"Yo, I need your shit for the wrap!" Nakiy yelled out while standing on the top tier.

"I got you, bro. Give me a second," Worlds replied. "Check to the better. I'm a let you dig your own grave."

"Ten!" Rob said, challenging him. He threw his chips into the pile with the other chips, waiting for everyone to call him.

"I'm down!" Drew said, folding his hand.

"Me, too!" Sean followed.

"I'll call you," Worlds said as he put in his chips and then showed his hand. "I have a boat! Aces over kings!"

Rob smiled and then laid down his cards on the table for everyone to see.

"I have quads," he said, showing that he had four tens, which beat Worlds's full house. "I was trying to get you to bet more, but you didn't," he added, with a smirk.

"Fuck you, nigga!" Worlds yelled, knowing that he had just lost.

He got up from the table to go grab something out of his room. He wanted Rob to say some slick shit so he could beat his ass, but Rob didn't.

Nakiy walked over to Worlds's room and knocked on the door. Worlds invited him inside as he grabbed the soups, cheese, and meat out of his drawer.

2

"What else do you need besides this?" he asked, passing him the food.

"That's it! I have everything else. The water is boiling now. You gonna help me make it, or you still playing poker?"

"Yeah, I'm trying to take these white boys' money. Rob's winning right now, but I'm up on paper. Sean's crazy ass calls everything. He don't care if he loses or not!" Worlds said as he headed back to the game.

As he walked down the steps, Fredd came out of his room and said, "Donte, when you get a second, I need to holla at you for a minute."

"Stop calling me that, Andrew." Worlds smirked.

They both liked calling each other by their government names to make one another mad.

3

"Give me a few minutes so I can finish getting this easy money real quick."

"That's what I want to talk to you about, bro. I'm talking about some real money, not those soups y'all playing for right now," Fredd stated matter-of-factly.

Worlds continued playing poker for about another hour until everyone lost their chips except for him and Rob. They counted them up and played for the extras. Afterward, he went upstairs to talk with his Islamic brother about business.

"*As-salāmu 'alaykum*," Worlds greeted, with the words "peace be unto you" in Arabic. "My bad it took me so long, bro."

"*Wa alaikum salaam*. It's cool. I just got finished making salat, so you need to do the same," Fredd said.

4

"*Alhamdulillahi.* I will as soon as you tell me what's up!" Worlds replied, leaning on the sink.

"Well, you know I'm leaving this week sometime, and I have that number that the bull gave me to contact him when I touch on the work. I wanted to know if you were still trying to link up with him too, being that you might also be out. Plus, I wanted to know if he's a trustworthy nigga. We only met him in here, and you already know how niggas come to jail and be all they can be."

Worlds smiled because he understood where his man was coming from. Muthafuckas came to jail with Benzes and Lexuses out there, but couldn't even make a phone call or buy commissary.

"Bull is cool. I did some homework on him a

couple of days ago, and he's really getting a dollar out there. He even did what he said he was going to do and put money on my account. Did you check yours yet?"

"Naw! I was going to check it when I called my mom later on, but I'll check it now," Fredd said as the two walked over to the phone.

"Yo, E! Come here real quick!" Worlds yelled up to Nakiy's room.

"Hold on, ock. I'm chiefing this shit up right now. I'll be down in a few minutes," he hollered out.

Fredd hung up the phone and gave Worlds the thumbs up, indicating that his money was also on there. "That nigga did what he said he would. So I guess he's definitely official. Now I hope he really puts us on when we get out so we can get this bread.

6

That brings me back to the question I asked you, are you down or what?"

"Damn right I'm down! As long as they drop my case when I go to court, I should be out of this bitch!" Worlds told his friend. "How much are we gonna get from him?"

"I'm trying to take whatever he gives us. I know between Philly and Chester, we should be able to move a large amount of it."

"I was under the presumption that you were going to chill out until you get out of rehab," Worlds questioned.

"My lawyer said that I don't have to go now. I just needed to give them an address so I can get released. I presented it to my PO, and she approved it already," Fredd said, with a smile on his face. It was just a waiting process now for him.

Worlds had met Fredd when he came on the block two months ago, and they had hit it off instantly. He considered him to be a very close friend. Not only was he a friend, but he was also Worlds's brother in faith. They all were. It was Nakiy who had piqued Worlds's interest about the Islamic religion. Worlds was already Muslim, but he had stopped practicing a while ago. Now he was back on his *deen* and going strong.

The three of them prayed five times a day together and went to *jum`ah* every Friday. They tried to make *taleem* as much as possible, but sometimes they wouldn't call it for their block. Other than that, they were very loyal and dedicated to their belief.

Each one of them had their Quran and prayer rug so they could pray in the confinement of their respective cells.

Worlds was locked up for getting pulled over with a gun in his car. He was on his way home from seeing some girl in Prospect Park, when he ran a stop sign. He didn't see the cop parked in the lot across the street. He tried to hide the gun under the seat, but due to him not having a license, it gave them probable cause to search the vehicle. Next thing he knew, he was in Delaware County Prison, being charged with possession of a firearm.

Fredd was in the house with his girlfriend, counting perks when his PO unexpectedly showed up. He tried to hide the pills, but it was too late. When he went in front of his black judge, he said that he had a problem and was using. They gave him six months and told him he would have to be in a rehab center. He hired a lawyer, and now he would be going straight home instead.

Nakiy's situation was simple: he let his girl put him in prison. She lied to his PO and said he hit her. Of course the PO believed her. Now Nakiy was sitting in jail waiting for everything to work itself out.

"Okay! Well, hit him up when you get out and set shit up. When I come home, we will get this money. Before that, though, there are a few loose ends I need to tighten up," Worlds stated, thinking about some friends that had fucked him over.

"What's that, bro?"

"Just some niggas out there running off at the mouth about shit. I can't let that slide. My BM gave me the rundown on a couple of them, so they gonna get it first. Those niggas on Turkey time right now."

"I'm here if you need me, but let's get this money, and when we see them, we'll deal with it accordingly," Fredd replied.

"Okay, well I'm about to call Dom before they lock us in. She's supposed to come tomorrow. *Assalamu 'alaikum.*"

"*Wa alaikum salaam.* I'm about to go play chess for awhile," Fredd said, heading over to the chess table.

* * *

A week later, Fredd was sitting in the holding cell waiting to be escorted up the hill to the bus stop. He was finally being discharged, and he couldn't wait to feel the freedom that was just a few moments away. For the past couple of days, he had been preparing himself mentally for what he was going to do.

"Grab your shit and let's go!" the CO yelled, heading for the van.

Fredd and eight other inmates followed the CO, trying to hurry up and get out of that place. Once they got in the van, everyone felt a sense of relief. They had seen many people get so close to leaving, but then a detainer or warrant popped up on them and kept them there. That's why no one was safe until they were outside of the wired fence.

When they reached the bus stop, they all exited the van and headed for the awaiting bus. Fredd was just about to get on the bus, when he heard his name being called and the sound of a horn.

"Yo, Fredd!" the voice said.

Fredd stepped back to see who was calling him. When he looked at the approaching car, he smiled at the driver, then walked over to the passenger side and hopped in.

"What's up, cannon? What are you doing here?"

"I came to pick up Drew, but he not getting out until tomorrow. I just got the text from his people. I was leaving when I saw you," Riggs stated.

"Damn, I'm glad to see you. I didn't want to be on the bus looking like this."

"What happened to your clothes?" Riggs said, noticing that he still had on blues.

"I don't know. They couldn't find my fucking bag, so they told me to leave this shit on. That had me hot, dawg."

"Well, here! Spark that shit up!" he said, passing him the Dutch filled with loud.

"That's what the fuck I'm talking about. I hope this is some good shit," Fredd said while lighting it up.

"I don't fuck with no bullshit, homie. You should know that by now. Matter of fact, you might need this," Riggs said, reaching inside the glove compartment and pulling out a silver .40 cal.

"What this for?" Fredd cocked it back, seeing if one was in the chamber.

"Till you get back on your feet. I thought you might need it just in case niggas act stupid out here.

14

I have to stop by my crib real quick, and then I'll take you home," Riggs said, pulling into the apartment complex. "You can come up, bro."

Fredd followed Riggs into the building and up to the second floor. As they walked up the steps, he heard a commotion coming from what sounded like Riggs's apartment. As Riggs was about to open the door, they could hear two voices.

"Bitch! Where is the stash at, for the last time, or I'm gonna kill your friend!" the masked man said.

His partner had the girl's friend on her stomach, with a gun to her head. She was scared to death and didn't know what to do. They had just returned from shopping, when they were ambushed and forced into the apartment.

"I'm telling you the truth. I don't know where my husband keeps the stuff. I just came to pick up some money from him to go shopping later," she said hysterically.

"I'm tired of playing with these bitches!" the other dude said as he then pulled the trigger.

Boc!

The shot went straight through her back. Then he pulled out a knife and repeatedly plowed it into her. She never had a chance.

"Noooo!" the girl screamed, trying to get to her friend, but she was restrained by a swift punch to the face by the other guy. The force of the blow sent her back onto the couch.

"Silence that bitch, and let's get the fuck out of here!"

16

When Riggs and Fredd heard the shot, they pulled out their guns. Riggs didn't know if it was his wife or not, but he had to get in there. He slowly opened the door, and they could see the man with his gun aimed at the unconscious girl on the couch.

Boom! Boom! Boom!

Blaca! Blaca! Blaca!

The shots found their marks, entering both intruders' bodies.

Riggs was the first to reach the area where the two goons had fallen. He gave both of them head shots before checking on his wife.

"Alexia, are you okay, baby?" he said, holding her in his arms.

"Yo! We have to get out of here before the cops come. You know the neighbors called them," Fredd said, looking over at Riggs.

"I'll get her out of here. Can you go into the bathroom and grab the shit under the mattress?" Riggs asked.

Fredd ran into the room, and when he lifted up the mattress, he couldn't believe his eyes. There were two packages wrapped up. Just by looking, he could tell that it was heroin. Right next to it were bundles of money. It looked like it was easily close to fifty grand. A bunch of thoughts started fluttering through his head as he grabbed the drugs and money, placing it inside of two pillow cases. As he was leaving, something caught his attention, making him think about what he was about to do.

Two

"Hold up! Wait a minute! Y'all thought I was finished? When I bought that Aston Martin, y'all thought it was rented. Flexin' on these niggas, I'm like Popeye on his spinach!" Meek Mill blared through the speakers as Torey and Zy cruised down 95 heading for Philly.

"After we drop off this work to young bull, let's go see what's up with those niggas on that block off of Woodland Avenue," Zy said.

"You talking about Divinity Street?" Torey asked.

Zy nodded his head yes.

"Those niggas never have any work out there. Whoever they worked for must not have a connect. We should just get a squad to run through there and take it over."

"Let's just put out some samples first to let the fiends know that we got it. Then we'll see what it do!" Zy replied.

"That's cool, but fuck these niggas! They probably soft-ass young bulls."

"You need to stop thinking like that. These young bulls are the ones out here busting their guns, raising the murder rate. So you need to watch out for them. They're trying to get their reps up. If we do that, we better be ready to lay everybody down," Zy said.

Torey lifted up his shirt, exposing his desert eagle that was tucked into his waistband.

"I'm always on go, my nigga. If they pull out, they better get the drop on me first, or they will become another casualty of the streets." He smirked.

"I feel you, cannon. I just want you to be ready for whatever. Now pass me the Amsterdam in the back seat. I'm trying to get fucked up by the time we get there. My aim is on point when I feeling it!"

"Say less," Torey agreed.

He took a swig of the liquor and then paused before passing it over to his homie.

By the time they made it to Philly, they were loud and fucked up off the liquor. As soon as they turned on the block, they could see all the fiends in line waiting to cop their fix for the day. Zy pulled up in front of the door and rolled down the passenger-side window.

"Yo, homie! Come holla at me real quick," Torey told one of the young boys. He couldn't have been more than fifteen years old.

"Give me a sec, cannon. I have to grab your bread," he replied, running up the street to the spot where they kept the cash.

Their crew was told never to keep the work and money in the same spot. That way, if they were robbed or got raided, they would only lose one or the other. He came back with a black plastic bag and jumped in the back seat.

"What took y'all so long to get here? You called three hours ago," Lil Rel stated.

"Business," Zy answered. "Is it all here? The last payment was short."

"Yeah, it's all there, plus what we owe from the last one," he said confidently.

Torey counted the money to make sure. After that, they passed him a package. Lil Rel smiled and tucked it under his shirt.

"I'll have something for you in a couple of days," Rel told them before exiting the car.

"Yo!" Torey said to Rel before he ran off.

Rel turned around to see what he wanted. He passed him a smaller package.

"Put that out on the streets as a tester, and let us know what it does."

"What is it?" Rel asked while looking inside.

"It's some new shit that we want to see how it sells. If everything is good, we'll be switching."

"Okay, let me get back to the money," he said walking off.

"That's right! It's all about the money!" Torey said as they pulled off.

The dope they gave Rel was all the same. The only difference was the samples were loaded with not only Quad 9 and Bonita, but also fentanyl. Zy suggested that they try something new, but never did Torey think that he meant that way. With the chemicals that it was mixed with, the wrong dose would surely kill its user.

Their next stop was the street in the southwest area that they were talking about. The block was dead as hell, except for a couple of stragglers who were walking around. They parked in the middle of the block and just observed for a while. They wanted to see who the dealers were and what they sold. After

about an hour, only a few people had come through

to cop.

"I don't know about this block, bro!" Torey said.

"It seems slow, but I really think we can move a

lot of work here. All we have to do is build up the

clientele, and we're set," Zy told him.

"If you say so! I'm rocking with you regardless.

I was just saying that we should hold off. Let's see

what the blocks around this one are doing, and then

we can get an idea of what we're up against," Torey

replied.

They drove around checking out the area, and

they realized that 52nd Street all the way to 54th and

Woodland was jumping. They decided the best thing

to do was put a little work out and built it from the bottom up.

"Let's go check out those bitches we met the other day in South Philly." Zy smiled.

"The ones from 27th and Tasker?"

"Yeah. Those bitches were bad. All they want to do is smoke with us, and I know we fucking!"

"That's all it is. Then I'ma hit them up and see where they at. Hopefully they don't try to set us up. You know how those South Philly girls are," Zy stated as they headed over the Gray's Ferry Bridge.

"This is the wrong time for niggas to try us. My trigger finger is itching," Torey replied.

Even though he was smiling, he really was trying to catch wreck. It had been a while since they had been in a shootout. They were both born in Philly but

26

moved to Delaware when they were ten years old.

Their parents were trying to get them away from the

violence, but that only made them hungrier for it. Zy

had caught his first shooting at the age of twelve. He

was defending Torey from a bully in school. From

that day on, he would start trouble with all the thugs

in his neighborhood, trying to get a rep.

Torey only toughened up because Zy kept

pushing him to fight whoever they had beef with.

Now he would bust his gun in the blink of an eye.

What they both didn't know was that those young

bulls in South Philly were on the same type of time

they were. They stayed on go and didn't care who

caught a slug.

They pulled up on the corner of 27th and Tasker

and waited for the chicks to come. Both of them had their guns sitting on their laps, with the safeties off. The girls came to the corner a couple minutes later looking for the guys. They spotted the bombed-out Pontiac Grand Prix and walked toward it.

Torey and Zy said "Damn!" at the same time when they saw what they were wearing.

Nydiyah was wearing a pair of tights that made her ass bounce more than it should. It jiggled even more because she wasn't wearing any panties. Her T-shirt made her perky D-cup breasts sit up straight. She was short, brown skinned, and very pretty.

Her friend Mya was average in the face, tall, and had a yellow complexion. Her hair came down her back. She didn't have a phat ass like Nydiyah, but it was enough to stick out the tennis skirt she was

28

rocking. Her DD breasts were trying to break free from their hold in the tank top she had on.

They hopped into the backseat, and Zy turned around just in time to see in between Mya's legs. She had on a pair of pink lace panties. Her pussy lips were screaming for attention, poking out of them. That made his dick hard.

"What's good with y'all?" Zy asked.

"Shit! Tryin' to get high. Y'all got some loud?" Nydiyah inquired, smacking the gum she was chewing.

"Yeah! Where we going to smoke?" Torey asked, holding up the Ziploc bag with the loud in it.

Their eyes lit up at the sight of the trees. They looked at each other and smiled.

"My people is out until tonight. We can go to my crib and blow," Mya told them.

"That's cool, but what time they coming back, 'cause I was going to grab a bottle too so we can chill a while."

"They won't get home from the casino until around four in the morning."

"Let's go, then. Where do you live?" Zy asked.

"I live on Dover Street. It's two blocks up and then make a right," she told him.

Zy pulled out into traffic and drove up to Mya's block. When they pulled up in front of her crib, Zy and Torey were on alert, just in case. Seeing that the block seemed so peaceful, they relaxed.

"Come on in, y'all. Did you get any Dutches?" Nydiyah asked while getting out of her car.

"I got four games and a couple of cigarillos, so we can roll all of them up!" Torey announced.

They walked behind the girls, thinking how they were going to fuck the shit out of them tonight. Zy pointed to the one he wanted, and Torey laughed because he wanted the same one. When they walked into the house, the only light they saw was the flickering of the television.

"Y'all can sit at the table and roll up, and I'll be right back," Mya said as she headed upstairs.

Nydiyah turned on the kitchen light and then followed her friend up the stairs.

"I can't wait to bend that ass up!" Zy said, pulling out the bag of trees as they started breaking the Dutches open.

"I don't care who I get as long as the pussy is good. If it's trash, I'ma let her know. You know I'm ignorant as hell!" Torey chuckled.

"You're wild, dawg!"

Nydiyah and Mya came back downstairs, and they all sat in the living room sparking up their Dutches. Mya turned the channel on the flat screen to *Empire* and they chilled, geeking off of the gay son messing with his new manager. By the time the show was over, they were fucked up.

"Y'all want us to dance?" Nydiyah asked.

She turned to one of the music channels and turned up the volume.

"Is she fucking with me, 'cause I'm fucking with you. I'm really in these streets, so what am I to do? I don't want you to leave, but if I gotta choose. I gotta keep it all the way a hundred, baby. I ain't got no time for you," PMB Rock played as the girls began dancing with one another.

Mya was so close that she could smell the Doublemint gum on Nydiyah's breath. Without saying a word, she kissed her softly on the lips. Nydiyah was hesitant at first, but she decided to play along with her friend. She had never experienced a sexual encounter with another woman before, so this was a first. She tongued Mya back passionately, and to her surprise, she felt her pussy getting wetter by the second. Her body was trembling with curiosity.

Zy and Torey peeped what was going on and started getting ready for the show. Just as the girls started taking off their clothes, Torey saw a shadow creeping down the stairs. He quickly reached for his gun that was tucked in the side of the couch. Zy picked up on his partner's movement and did the same.

Before the guy coming downstairs could raise his gun, Zy had the drop on him.

Boc! Boc!

Two shots hit him, one in the leg and one in his arm in which he was carrying the gun.

Nydiyah screamed at the sound of the gunfire.

"Shut the fuck up, bitch!" Torey said, pointing the gun at them.

Nydiyah instantly quieted up. Tears were coming down her face as she stood there scared. On the other hand, Mya wasn't scared at all, which meant that she was the one who had tried to set them up.

"So you tried to set us up, bitch!" Torey smacked her across the head with the butt of his gun. She hit the floor face first. Zy walked up on the nigga and hit him close range three times in the chest.

"Put that scheming bitch to sleep!" Zy told Torey.

Torey shot Mya in the head and again in the chest. He then turned the gun on Nydiyah, who was shaking uncontrollably.

"I, I didn't know nothing about this," she sniffled.

For some reason, Zy believed her and walked over to Torey.

"Come on, man. Let the bitch be. We have to get up outta here," he whispered.

Torey grabbed her purse and took her ID out and looked at it.

"I know where you live. Keep your mouth shut, and you'll be okay."

They ran out of the house and jumped into their car, trying to get out of Dodge before the cops showed up. They got to I-76 in less than five minutes. Zy didn't take his foot off the gas until they were on I-95.

"Yo! You were on your shit, nigga!" Zy bragged.

Torey nodded his head in agreement as they headed back to Delaware. He put on his favorite song that they always played when niggas failed to get them.

"Stay schemin', niggas tryna get at me. I ride for my niggas."

36

Zy sparked one of the Dutches they rolled earlier and took a couple of swigs. He passed it over to Torey, who was trying to make sure they weren't being followed. It was just something they always did. They never knew when a good Samaritan would try to take them until the cops caught up to them. He hit the Dutch and relaxed.

"Turn up that shit, homie! That's my shit!" Zy said, cruising to the music.

Torey turned it up, and they both felt good about not getting caught slipping.

"It's funny when these stars get to acting like their broads, and every nigga's squad don't come deep with niggas like ours."

Three

"What looked like a robbery gone bad has left two people dead and one traumatized. We are standing outside of this South Philly home on the fifteen hundred block of Dover Street," the reporter began, giving everyone who was watching the breaking news and all the details that had happened that night.

"Yo! Turn that up real quick. That's my block!" Reece shouted, trying to make it over to the television to catch what they were saying.

"Damn! They hit them up in the crib!" Walid said, holding the remote. "They left a survivor, though. They had to be some young niggas."

"I know the two people that stay at that crib. They were brother and sister, but they were some grimy muthafuckas, real talk!" Reece said as he walked away from the television.

Reece was in Graterford doing time for an armed robbery that he didn't commit. He had been walking home from the McDonald's on Gray's Ferry, when two masked men ran past him and dropped a bag. He picked it up and found a gun along with money, and just as he tried to tuck it, two cops rode upon him. They found the evidence and locked him up.

Being from the hood, Reece knew the code of the streets, so he wouldn't say anything. They found him guilty and gave him ten to twenty years. He knew that he would beat it on appeal, so he was just waiting for his moment to get back on the streets. Someone sent him a birdie letting him know who did it. They took care of him for not saying anything, and even paid for his appeal lawyer. They also told him that they had him when he got home.

"You making the wraps tonight, or we going to eat a chee chee?" Walid asked.

"We can do the wraps. Just bring your stuff out, and I'll grab mine. We gotta hurry up though 'cause the game come on in a few."

"I know. I took Cleveland tonight. It's no way they're gonna go down 3-0 in Cleveland. Lebron is not having that!"

"You're crazy! The Splash brothers ain't even put on a show yet. What you think gonna happen once they start hitting? Cleveland might lose by forty this time!" Reece smiled.

"I got ten soups on Cleveland," Walid replied.

"That's a bet!" he stated.

They shook hands and went to prepare their meal before they had to lock in at nine o'clock.

* * *

Worlds was at Media waiting to see the judge. He was sitting in the holding cell eating the egg salad sandwich they were given when they first walked in. He and A.J. were hopefully about to get their cases thrown out.

A.J. was Worlds's baby mom's brother. They met through her when he used to always come over. Now they were like family.

"I hope we make it back before visits start. My mom is gonna bring my son up," A.J. said.

"Is they riding with Dom?"

"She said she was. I just want to see my lil man. Hopefully I will be out of here today."

41

"Me too. Then we won't have to get a visit. There goes your PD right there," Worlds replied.

"I hope he has some good news for me. I'm not going to take anything unless it's time served."

A.J.'s PD came over to talk to him. When they were finished, the DA wanted to give him one to two years for each count running wild. That made him so mad. He told his lawyer that he would rather go to trial, and his lawyer walked away.

Worlds's case was thrown out because the witnesses didn't show up again. The judge left the room for the prosecutor to recharge him once they got their shit together. They headed back to Delaware County Prison right after that.

Worlds couldn't wait to get back to the streets. He had a lot of catching up to do. He hoped they released him tonight since it was still early, but it didn't matter as long as he was going home. Then he remembered that his PO still had to lift his detainer, which shouldn't be a problem being that they had dropped his case.

* * *

Fredd was on Lancaster Avenue sitting in Texas Wiener eating breakfast, when Robert Sean, Terrance, and Chubb walked in. They all sat at a table right across from him. He knew who they were, but was wondering if they knew who he was. From the looks of it, they didn't or just didn't care. He got off the stool and approached them.

"You mind if I sit here?" he asked.

The three men looked up and stared at Fredd for a minute.

"What's up, cannon. Do we know you?" Chubb said, sizing him up.

"It's Fredd, fat boy. I used to live right up the street from you."

"I don't remember you, homie. So kick rocks!" Chubb replied in an aggressive tone.

Not wanting to start drama inside the restaurant, Fredd started walking away from the table.

"Bring your ass back over here, bitch boy!" Robert Sean said with a smirk on his face.

Fredd turned around, and all three men were laughing at him. He smiled and sat down with them. They all gave him a fist bump and head nod.

"Where the hell have you been, nigga? You don't fuck with us bottom boys no more?" Chubb asked.

"I've been booked, and before that, I was trying to stay out of the way."

"What brings you back around here?" Terrance inquired.

"I'm trying to get a team together 'cause I'm about to come up on a nice amount of work," he boasted.

"So what, you trying to be a boss now?" Robert Sean asked.

He remembered Fredd as being the nigga always sitting on the porch drinking beer. Now he was trying to get them to work for him.

"Naw! I need you niggas to run shit for me out here while I handle shit in Sharon Hill and out in Chester. We can all eat off of this. Y'all wit it or what?"

"So why do you need us? What's to stop us from just taking your shit and keeping it for ourselves?" Chubb asked.

Chubb never liked Fredd, even when he used to live around the same area. Fredd and him were fucking the same broad, and Chubb got mad when she chose Fredd over him. The hatred had gotten to the point where Chubb wanted to rock him, but he didn't want to go out like that over a bitch.

"Look, man, y'all niggas been out here hustling in these streets since we were young bulls. I don't really have experience with dope, but you do. I know you're tired of nickels and dimes. I'm trying to put you on to some real bread. It's every hustler's dream to be caked up, and I'm offering you that opportunity."

"So where are you going to get this work from?"
Terrance wondered.

"My man that I was locked up with came home
and lives out in Florida with his wife. He's gonna
front me and some bull named Worlds a couple of
joints on consignment. All we have to do is show him
that we can get this money in a reasonable amount of
time. I'm just waiting for my nigga to come home
now."

"When are you getting them?" Chubb questioned, thinking dollar signs in his head.

"It won't be for a couple of weeks. For now,
though, I have a sweet lick that we can eat off of. He
holding shit. We can take some of the money from
that and get some other shit until then."

"So who we jacking 'cause I need some bread right now?" Robert Sean asked.

They stayed in the restaurant for another half hour just going over everything. He ran the whole plan over and over again so they wouldn't forget. He knew they were hungry for a dollar, so it wouldn't be a problem getting them to do the lick.

* * *

"Hurry up with my shit! You know I have to be in the crib by ten o'clock!" Drew yelled in the kitchen to Riggs.

"I got you, bro. You won't be late!" he replied.

Riggs was watching Aubrey, a Spanish woman, bag up the last bundle of dope so he could give it to his man.

48

Drew had just come home three days ago and already was trying to get at some money. He had a few people left in his cell phone from before he went to prison, and he was trying to build back up.

Aubrey walked into the living room to bring Drew the bag with the bundles inside. She was only wearing a thong and a mouth protector because Riggs didn't trust her. Drew took the bag from her and squeezed her ass as she walked back into the kitchen.

"You gonna take the other car, or do I have to take you home?" Riggs asked.

"My girl is outside waiting for me, so I'm good. I'll be over here tomorrow morning to pick up some more."

They gave each other a half hug, and Drew left. The girl in the kitchen then walked over to Riggs and rubbed his crotch through his pants. His penis stood at attention, and he knew exactly what he needed. He sat down on the couch and told her to come over to him.

"Can I get a hit first? Then I will take care of you, papi," she said.

Riggs pulled out a needle, and Aubrey licked her lips at the sight of the liquid filling inside. She took off the rubber gloves she had on, and wrapped one around her arm so that a vein would pop up. Riggs watched as she shot the liquid into her arm, causing her to freeze as the sensation took over her body. She was now ready for action.

She kneeled between his legs and took his dick into her mouth. The warmth of her mouth had him ready to explode. She made his dick make popping noises as she moved her head up and down while jerking on it at the same time. Riggs lasted as long as he could before shooting all of his load into her mouth.

"Are you satisfied, papi?" she moaned.

"I sure am! Now let's get out of here. I have to go pick up your sister from work."

She rushed and got dressed so they could leave. Riggs wanted to stop over at Fredd's crib before he picked up Alexia. That's why he needed to leave, or else he would have stayed and fucked Aubrey for the great head she had just given him.

He dropped off Aubrey and then stopped over at Fredd's place. When he pulled up, Fredd was sitting on the porch talking on his cell phone. Riggs parked and walked up onto the porch.

"What's up with you, nigga?" Fredd said, giving him a handshake.

"Shit! Just came to holla at you real quick. Good looking out on that shit the other day. I'm glad you were with me."

"That wasn't about shit! You're my man, dawg. I got your back."

"Let's go in the crib. I have to show you something," Riggs said as they both headed inside.

Riggs pulled out a bag with around four hundred bundles and passed it to Fredd.

"What's this for, bro?"

"I was hoping you could handle that for me, and you can keep twenty-five percent of what you, make," Riggs told him.

Fredd started adding it up in his head and realized that it wasn't a lot of money. It would only be $6,000 while Riggs would pull in $18,000. But Fredd decided it would do for now.

"That's cool with me. I'll let you know when I have some green for you to pick up, bro," Fredd said.

"Alright. I have to go pick up wifey. I'll get at you tomorrow sometime."

When Riggs left, Fredd laughed at the fact that he was now being treated like the worker instead of a partner.

Not for long. Not for long at all! he thought to himself.

Four

"So you didn't tell anybody that I was home, did you?" Worlds asked as they rode down Baltimore Pike.

His PO had finally gotten him released after letting him sit an extra couple of days. The PO thought he was teaching Worlds a lesson, but instead, that only made him want to get at niggas even more. His so-called friends had crossed him. Even his baby mom, who he thought loved and worshiped the ground that he walked on, deceived him by sleeping with his man. Retribution was only a short time away.

"No! I didn't say anything to anybody, nigga! You're mine for the first forty-eight hours, and then you can go see your little friends," Dom replied.

When Dominique first got World's call that he was getting out, she was somewhat excited and scared. She was excited that he was coming home, but she was afraid that he would try to shit on her like her baby father did when he came home. Dominique's problem was that she cared too much for people. She would give you her heart if you needed it. However, it seemed that the more she gave, the more people treated her poorly. She hoped that his time wasn't going to be like that. She really loved Worlds and wanted a life together with him.

"You know I got you, so stop looking at me like that. Did you bring what I asked?"

She pointed under the passenger seat. Worlds reached underneath and smiled as he felt the handle to his Glock 9 mm. He lifted it up, cocked it to make sure one was in the chamber, and then put it back beneath the seat.

"Did you do the other thing I told you to do?" he then asked, sticking his hand between her thighs, feeling her panty-less pussy.

It was shaved bald and felt smooth. She giggled and moaned at the same time as he stuck two fingers inside, making her wet. He pulled his soaked fingers out and tasted her sweet juices.

"You gonna make me crash before we get home?" she whispered, enjoying his touch.

"You need to hurry up. I got something for you!" he said, putting her hand on his dick.

She rubbed it and felt him get super hard, which only made her pussy get even wetter.

56

When they got to Dom's house, Worlds took a shower to wash off the prison scent, only to add a more enticing scent—the scent of sex. They fucked for hours until he couldn't take any more. They gave each other what they both so desperately needed. Like the lyrics of Chris Brown's song says, "Worlds sexed her to sleep."

Worlds woke up around 11:00 p.m. He wanted to catch up to a couple of niggas before Dom woke up looking for him. He eased out of bed, grabbed her car keys, and hit the streets. Everybody that shit on him while he was down was about to feel his pain.

He pulled up to the corner of Pine Lane and saw a couple of familiar faces, but not the one he was looking for.

"What's good, nigga?" he said, rolling down his window.

They all stared for a minute, until one of them who recognized him spoke up.

"Ain't shit! When you get out of that hell hole?"

"Earlier today. Did you see that nigga Trap today?"

"Yeah. He up the street talking to some bitch at the Chinese store. You good?" Bubb stated, sensing something was up.

"Yeah. I'm straight. But if you hear something, it's only me."

Bubb knew exactly what he was talking about. He gave him a head nod and finished the conversation with the young boys on the corner. Bubb was one of Chester's most ruthless killers. He

58

already beat multiple homicides, and he wasn't afraid to bust his gun at whoever, or whenever.

Worlds headed in the direction of the Chinese store. When he pulled up, Trap had his back toward him, talking to a girl he was with. Worlds jumped out of the car and walked over to them.

"Yo, Trap. What's good, my nigga? Let me holla at you for a sec," he said.

Trap turned around, and when he saw who it was, he got nervous. He didn't know if he should start begging for his life or run. He decided to run, but he didn't make it far. Worlds pulled out his gun and shot him in the back. The girl tried screaming, but caught one right between the eyes. She died before she hit the ground. Worlds ran up to Trap, who was bleeding out, and hit him again in the back of the head. Worlds

got in the car and peeled off to his next destination.

He pulled up past his man's crib and parked on

the side street. He exited the vehicle and walked

down the street, making sure no one was out before

he knocked on the door. When Gotti answered the

door, he stared down the barrel of a gun.

"What's up, nigga? You thought I wasn't gonna

find out about you fucking my BM. Back the fuck

up!" Worlds blurted out.

Gotti held his hands up and backed up into the

house. He didn't know what to do.

"Where is the work and the money?" he

questioned, knowing that Gotti was getting at a

couple of dollars.

"It's not here, man, and I didn't know y'all were still together. I wouldn't never disrespect you like that," Gotti lied.

Gotti knew they were together because he had seen her come up to visit Worlds when he was on visits with his mom. When Gotti got out, he saw Amanda and told her that Worlds had three other girls coming to see him every week. She got mad and tried to get back at him by sleeping with Gotti. Afterward, she told Worlds what she did, trying to ask for forgiveness, but he told her to fuck off.

"She told me all about the shade you threw my way. I would have never done that shit to you, dawg! Now I'm gonna ask you one more time. If you want to live, where is the shit at?"

Thinking he would be better off giving it to Worlds, Gotti showed him where the money and work was. He just wanted to live to see another day. He could get that little bit of shit back in no time. Worlds put the stuff in a plastic shopping bag, and he then made Gotti sit in a chair in his kitchen.

"Where is the rest of it, 'cause I know you had more," Worlds asked.

"That's it, man! I just gave the plug his money a couple of hours ago. He was supposed to drop off something in the morning."

Worlds stuck the gun under Gotti's chin and threatened, "You better not be lying to me, nigga!"

Gotti just wanted to get out of the situation. He was gonna kill Worlds when he had the chance.

However, he wouldn't get the chance, as Worlds blew his brains all over the ceiling and walls. Brain matter flew everywhere. Some blood even got on his clothes. He didn't care. Worlds rushed out of the house and headed back to Dom's crib. She was still sleeping, so he eased back into bed like he had never left.

The next morning when he woke up, he counted the money and drugs. There was only $535 and around ten ounces of loud. Worlds was pissed, but he didn't care as long as that nigga was swimming with the fish. Besides, he soon had big plans with Fredd. It was time to start making money.

* * *

Zy and Torey were sitting in the Fresh Grocer parking lot waiting for their connect to arrive. They had set up the meeting about a week ago, and he agreed to give them a little extra of whatever they copped.

"This nigga always late, man. We need to find a better connect," Torey said, taking a puff off the loud he was smoking.

"I know, but right now he's all we got because of the drought. I did hear about some niggas down the bottom, about to come up on a good plug."

"Who you hear that from 'cause I damn sure would like to meet whoever it is."

"Some bitch said this nigga she knew told her over pillow talk that he was about to make major moves. You know niggas can't hold water when some bitch put it on them," Zy chuckled. "If you want, we can get her to set that nigga up so we can take his shit."

"I'm with it! Let me know when," Torey agreed.

A black A7 Audi pulled up beside them and rolled down the window. Zy had his finger on the trigger in a flash, but relaxed when he saw who it was.

"What I tell you about pulling up on niggas like that? You almost got hit up again!" Zy threatened.

"You ain't hitting nothing but one of those skeezers y'all be fucking with!" Jose answered.

They all laughed and got out of their cars.

Jose gave them the bag with the one hundred bundles in it. They gave him the $3,000 and shook hands.

"I gave you the best deal I could do right now. It's fucked up out here. We need some mules that can go straight to the plug and grab the raw and uncut!" Jose said seriously.

"What about the extra you said?"

"Oh yeah, I forgot!" Jose said as he reached inside the car and gave them another twenty bundles. "That's on me, bro. I'll let y'all know if I can get my shipment here in the next couple days. If you don't hear anything from me, hit my jack."

"Cool! Be safe, you taco-eating muthafucka!" Torey joked.

Jose gave him a crazy look before leaving. They had some more work, but they needed more. They decided to see about the nigga that the chick was talking about.

* * *

Fredd was sitting in the car talking to Riggs about how the dope was selling on the block. They were so into their conversation that they didn't see the three hooded figures until it was too late.

"You niggas know what time it is? Don't fucking move, and you might just walk up outta here!" the first one said, with his gun aimed at Riggs's head.

"What's this all about? We don't have shit!" Riggs pleaded. He was pissed off because he let some niggas get the drop on him. He was usually on point.

"Shut the fuck up! Get out of the car slowly and give us the work and money, and you'll live," the second man told them.

He opened the passenger-side door and dragged out Fredd. The hooded man on the driver's side did

67

the same thing to Riggs while the third man searched for the work.

He found it in a small duffel bag. He grabbed it and nodded to his two partners. They started backing away, when Riggs had something to say.

"When I find out who you are, I'm gonna kill you myself and feed your bodies to my pits."

They all stopped and looked at each other. The man with the duffel bag lifted his gun up and aimed at Riggs. Riggs didn't even flinch. He just grilled the guy the whole time.

Boc! Boc!

The shots hit Riggs in the chest, and he fell up against the car.

One of the other men pointed his gun at Fredd and squeezed the trigger. But the gun didn't go off.

They ran away, leaving Fredd and his wounded friend. Fredd rushed over to the other side of the car to check on Riggs. He was just lying there, so Fredd thought he was dead. He hopped in the driver's seat and peeled off, leaving Riggs there bleeding to death.

When they got far enough away, they removed their hoodies and gave each other a pound.

"We did that shit! I didn't think you were going to shoot the nigga, though!" Terrance said, looking into the duffel bag. "I don't know how much it is, but it looks like a lot."

"I should have hit that punk-ass nigga Fredd for being so disrespectful," Chubb replied.

"You need to leave that nigga alone. He didn't do anything to your ass. As long as he doesn't open his mouth to the cops, we're cool. If he does say anything, then we'll also put his ass to sleep."

"Do you even know where you're going? You've passed the damn exit, nigga!" Chubb said, making them all laugh.

"Fuck! We'll just get off at the next exit and cut through the park. We have to get rid of this car anyway. I'm glad we didn't take your sister's car," Robert Sean stated as they got off at the next exit.

"She would have been pissed, especially if someone seen us leaving the scene and took down the license plate number," Terrance told them.

Once they got rid of the car, they went to Chubb's crib on 71st and Haverford Avenue. That way they could have peace and quiet as they counted the dope

70

and money. While they were counting the money, someone knocked on the door.

"Who the fuck is that?" Terrance whispered.

Chubb got up and peeked through the curtain to see who it was. After confirming the person's identity, Chubb unlocked the door. He stepped to the side, allowing Fredd to enter.

"What the fuck did you have to shoot him for?" he asked, ice-grilling Chubb because he knew he was the one who pulled the trigger.

"That nigga disrespected me, so he got what he deserved. Don't nobody threaten me," Chubb replied, letting Fredd know not to even try it.

Terrance tried to calm the storm that was brewing: "Look! We got the money and the work, so let's get paid."

He emptied the duffel bag out on the table. Fredd relaxed and smiled, thinking that he had just hit a good lick. Now all he had to do was count everything and give them the work to sell.

"I'll keep that little bit of cash and whatever y'all make with the dope. We'll split it four ways," Fredd told them, reaching for the money.

"No the fuck you won't! We split everything just like we agreed from the beginning!" Robert Sean stated.

"It's only around $19,000 there. That was some for the money he was going to give to the plug tonight. It's a lot more once we sell the dope," Fredd said.

"Good! We'll all split that, and then once this work is gone, we'll all be sitting a little nice. It looks like only a quarter of a brick anyway. If it's raw enough, we can cut it and almost get double its original value," Terrance told them, thinking in his head about the numbers.

They thought it would be more work than that.

Defeated, Fredd took his portion of the money and left. He wasn't happy at all about the outcome, but he wasn't going to argue either. He was outnumbered and outgunned three to one. He knew their business relationship wasn't going to last too long. He just wanted to get what he could out of them first. Once they locked up most of West Philly, he wouldn't need them anymore. They were just his pawns in a dangerous game of chess.

* * *

"Mmmmm, oh God, no!" Donte heard a noise coming from his mother's room, so he and his next door neighbor went to see if his mom was okay.

As they approached the door, he could hear what sounded like his mom crying.

"Momma, are you okay?" he called to her in a mild yell.

His friend peeked through the hole on the door. He could see a man holding down Donte's mom's hands while another man was sexually assaulting her.

"We have to call the cops and get your mom some help," he said as he pulled Donte away from the door.

Donte yanked away from his neighbor and rushed into his sister's room. The neighbor didn't

74

chase after him. Instead, he rushed downstairs and out the door so he could call for help.

Donte searched in his sister's closet until he found what he was looking for. He grabbed the black box and opened it. His sister's gun was still in there. Donte checked the clip, loaded it, and cocked one in the chamber. As he walked toward his mom's room, he heard the noise getting louder, and it sounded like one of the men was slapping her.

He pushed the door open and entered the room. The two men weren't even paying attention to him. They were caught up in their own desires.

"Leave my momma alone!" Donte yelled as tears ran down his cheeks.

One man looked up and saw the gun in his hand. He tapped his partner to get his attention. They both looked at Donte holding the gun on them.

"Lil nigga, give me that gun before I do the same thing to you as I'm doing to your bitch-ass mom!" one of the men said, getting off the bed and heading in Donte's direction.

Without any hesitation, Donte squeezed the trigger of the gun. The man walking toward him caught four of the bullets. The other man tried to charge at him but was hit with two of the next barrage of bullets.

"Donte!" his mom yelled, rushing over to him as he stared at the two bodies on the floor.

When she looked into his eyes, all she saw was a blank stare. Even his tears had stopped, and no other expression was visible. She covered herself with a sheet and tried to pull her son out of the room.

76

Donte was still holding the gun in his hand when the cops rushed into the house. He wasn't even scared or nervous about what he just had done. His mom was shaken up, but the two men who had raped her were dead.

"Worlds!" Dom yelled, shaking him and trying to wake him up.

He jumped up in a cold sweat. He was having another nightmare. That was his third one in the last week. He didn't understand why he was having them all of a sudden.

"Are you okay?" she asked. "You're sweating all over."

"Yeah! I'm good!" he replied, getting out of bed and heading into the bathroom.

He washed his face and looked in the mirror.

He was only eight years old when he first killed someone. From that day forth, he had become the menace he was today, and he didn't take shit from anyone.

He walked out of the bathroom and got back into bed with Dom. She slid over to him and lay on his chest. She knew what was going on because he had already talked to her about it.

"You know I love you, right?" she said, rubbing his arm.

"Oh yeah? So prove it to me then, sexy!" He smiled, pushing her head down toward his penis.

She gave him a naughty look, and then she showed him just how much. Donte lay back and enjoyed the show.

Five

Walid and Reece were transferred to SCI—Camp Hill—because they were being classified. Each one of them was hoping they would stay in their own region so their families wouldn't have to travel too far to see them.

They were sitting in the holding cell waiting to get a pair of blues from the inmate workers, when a CO walked up to them. Everybody only had on their shoes, socks, T-shirt, and briefs. The CO looked around at everybody and stopped when he saw an old white man with missing teeth.

"What time did you wake up this morning?"

The man looked at him for a second before replying, "Three. Why?"

"Your breath smells like mints, so I was wondering," he said, sniffing the air.

"Oh, okay."

"No! No! Like you meant to brush your teeth this morning," he said, getting a laugh from everybody.

The man just shook his head. Then he spotted another guy looking crazy, with his shirt tucked into his briefs.

"Hold on, man. I have a serious question for you. Why do you have your T-shirt tucked into your Supermans?" he asked. "What? You trying to bring sexy back? You know what I'm doing, right? I'm just bidding off you."

He had everybody laughing at his jokes.

Walid and Reece just sat in the back without saying anything. They wanted to get this over with so they could get to their cell and relax. Walid was hoping that his appeal would hurry up and come through. Reece already had over a year in, so he was just waiting on a green sheet from parole.

"These niggas are so crazy up here. I can't wait to get out!" Reece said to Walid.

"*Isha Allah*, we both will be out of here in a couple of months. I'm trying to get back to the streets. They calling for me out there," Walid answered.

"I feel you, bro. Maybe we can link up and do the damn thing once we out."

"Definitely, my nigga. You already know how I

get down. My brothers are out there holding shit down until I touch."

"Say no more, then!" Reece said.

Just like that, a bond was formed between the two men. Now it was just a matter of time before they would be home.

* * *

"Yo! This place is jumping, bro. We might have to come through here more often," Zy said, looking at all the females sitting or dancing in their seats with hardly any clothes on.

It was hot in there, so they took off the jackets they were wearing.

"Do you see the chick yet?"

Zy looked around and scanned the area for her,

but he didn't see anybody.

"Naw! I think they might be running late or something."

"We should have met him down the bottom. I don't know why he wanted to come here. Scooter's was right there at 38th and Lancaster."

"It's cool! Let's just order some drinks and holla at some of these broads while we wait," Zy said as he ordered a drink.

Fredd walked into the bar with the girl a couple minutes later. She pointed to the corner where Zy and Torey were standing.

"That's them right there. You gonna hook me up tonight, right?"

Stacy was from 40th and Brown. She was five

two, 140 pounds, and had a body out of this world.

She was thicker until she started using dope.

Everybody used to want to get at her, but she would

turn them all down. Now all you had to do was hold

up a couple of bags of heroin, and she'd suck the skin

off your dick.

"I said I got you if these niggas give me a good

offer. I didn't come here to leave empty-handed,"

Fredd replied, walking over to where the two men

were standing.

Torey and Zy watched as he and Stacy appro-

ached them. They looked at his appearance and

thought it was a joke. Fredd had on a pair of Guess

jeans and a Polo T-shirt.

"That nigga don't look like he's getting money

with that old-ass shit on." Zy smirked.

"Chill out, my nigga. Let's hear what he has to say first before we start judging."

"Okay. But if it's some bullshit, I'ma smoke his ass soon as he leaves this joint."

"What's up, fellas? Stacy tells me that you're trying to find a good connect. How much are you trying to grab?" Fredd asked.

"I'm not trying to discuss business here. You never know who's listening," Torey stated as he looked around.

"That's the reason I chose this place. The music is loud enough where we can talk regular, and no one can hear us unless they're right here."

Zy agreed after taking everything into consideration. He knew that Fredd was right, so he asked him a question. "How much work can you get at one time, and is it any good?"

"I can assure you that the quality is very good. I can let Stacy here prove it to you if you like," he said, holding up a bag so she could see it. "And I can get you whatever amount you need."

"Cool! Let her try it out then," Torey replied.

Stacy's mouth was watering at the thought of getting the high she'd been craving all night. Fredd passed it to her, and she scurried off toward the ladies' room. She already knew that it was some good dope, but Fredd had told her he would give her something, so he kept his word.

She returned from the bathroom ten minutes later.

Her eyes were half closed, and her speech was slurred as she told them how it was. "That is some good dope!"

She sat down in one of the chairs and was nodding in and out.

Zy and Torey smiled at each other thinking how they would come up off of this. They were even still going to mix it with the fentanyl for the extra boost. Fredd was also smiling, but not for the same reason. He was going to cut the dope he had, to be able to give them what they needed. Even though it was cut twice, he also knew that it would still have a lot of kick with the fentanyl.

"We want to start off with 400 bundles, if that's not too much for you." Torey smirked.

He thought Fredd wouldn't be able to get that amount of dope, which was actually a lot more than what they were able to get right now. They only had about 30 bundles left from the 120 they got from Jose. They tried to get more, but he wasn't able to right now.

"That's not a problem! Just have that money for me in a couple of days."

"I'll at least need until tomorrow, and I'll call you with the meeting spot. Is that cool with you guys?"

Torey and Zy had no choice but to agree. They needed work now because the new street was really starting to pick up now.

"Here's the number you can reach me at. Just call when you're ready to do business. I hope it's not much longer because we have plenty of buyers waiting," Zy said, passing him a piece of paper with his cell phone number on it.

Fredd took the paper, and they shook hands. Just like that, a deal had been made, and now it was up to Fredd to make sure he delivered.

He waited for another ten minutes after they had left before he left. He had to get back down the bottom and try to get whatever they were holding, because he needed that to go with what he had. He couldn't wait for his Florida plug to come through so he would be ready when Worlds got home. He knew that once Worlds was out, they would be unstoppable in the drug game.

He still was going to hit every lick that came his

way, with the help of his little crew he had formed.

What he didn't know was that Worlds was already

home. He was just lying low and making sure no one

would be on his ass before he got up with Fredd.

* * *

Worlds was sitting in the crib watching ESPN,

when he received a phone call. He picked up his

iPhone from off the nightstand and looked at the

screen.

"Yo, Bubb! What's good, my nigga?" he said,

answering it.

"Ain't shit. Can you talk right now?"

"Yeah. I was just watching this shit about Durant.

That nigga really just left OKC to go to Golden

State."

"Wouldn't you do that shit just to play with the Splash brothers?" Bubb stated. "Anyway, shit has been hot around here ever since you handled your business with ol' boy. I think somebody is talking, but they not saying you. They blaming it on some niggas from the Gardens, so, my nigga, you in the clear!"

"That's good to know. Now I can hit up my homie and get to the money. I was tired of sitting around the crib all day."

"Well just look out when you get some work. Shit has really been dry around here," Bubb stated.

"I have a little something for you right now if you want it. Come to my girl's spot in like twenty minutes."

"What is it?" Bubb questioned.

"Loud," Worlds answered, thinking about the work he took from Gotti.

"Okay, cool! But I'm talking real work. I'll see you in a few, 'cause I don't like speaking about shit on the jack."

"I feel you, and I'll get at you when you get here."

Worlds ended the call just in time to catch the end of *SportsCenter*. They were talking about how Lebron and Cleveland should try to sign D. Wade to help match up against the Warriors. They even mentioned Gasol's name too.

He laughed as he sipped on some Hennessy. He jumped when he heard the front door slam. A couple of seconds later, Dom walked in, staring at Worlds like she was ready to kill him.

"I thought you didn't fuck with your baby mom anymore?" she asked, throwing her keys at him, just missing his head.

"What are you talking about?"

"Don't fucking play dumb with me, Donte. I've stuck by you the whole time you were locked up, and this is how you repay me!" she said, pulling up something on her phone and showing it to him.

Worlds read the message that Amanda had posted on Facebook, and then Dom showed him the video of them on Snapchat.

She was so upset, tears started falling from her eyes. Worlds knew he had fucked up by taking pictures of him and his family. He didn't want to hurt Dom because she had done so much for him.

"Come here, baby. I'm sorry about that. I didn't know she was going to post that. All I did was go see my kids. You can understand that, can't you?" he asked, trying to calm down the situation.

"If you wanted to still be with her, why didn't you say so? I would have fell the fuck back. I feel like you were just using me for money."

Dominique was a good, ambitious twenty-five-year-old, but at that minute she felt like committing murder. People always took her kindness for weakness. Worlds tried to put his arms around her, but she pushed him away.

"Why would you do this to me?" she yelled.

"I told you, nothing's going on between us. If you don't believe me, then fuck it. I'm out of here!"

He started getting dressed and then headed for the door. Dom ran in front of him and blocked the entrance. She would not move out of his way.

"You're not going anywhere. You're gonna stay here and tell me what I want to know."

"Get out my way. I need some air!" he stated, pushing her to the side.

He walked out the door and headed up the street. He didn't have a car yet, so he just walked around for a while. Bubb pulled up alongside him and rolled down the window. "What's up, nigga? Where the hell you going?"

Worlds walked over to the car and hopped inside.

He leaned the seat back a little, pulled out the bag of loud, and passed it over to Bubb.

"I had to get out of the crib for a few. Dom's tripping about me going to the playground with my kids and their mother."

"Why she tripping about that? You gotta see your kids."

"Man, Amanda posted that shit on the 'Book and Snapchat. Now Dom thinks I'm still fucking her," Worlds replied.

"Damn, nigga! I know you're bloody about that. Well I'm going to the crib. Do you want to come chill and blow?"

"Naw! I'm about to go back home and get shit straight with her. Can you take me out to Philly tomorrow? I have to get up with the bull Fredd, so we can get shit poppin' out here. It's money to be made!" Worlds said.

"I got you. Just hit my jack when you're ready, and I'll swing through."

"Cool! I'll get at you then," he said, opening the door to get out.

"How much is this, and what you want back?" Bubb asked, holding up the package.

"It's ten ounces, and just give me $1,500 back, and you keep the rest. I have some bigger shit going on if you trying to really get at some money. I'll be linking up with a real plug in a day or two. That's why I need to get out to Philly!"

"Well, like I said, I need some work, so let me know what's up. I'm with you," Bubb said as he started to get excited.

"I'll hit you up in the a.m. then," Worlds said as he walked away toward his house.

It was time to get the money, and nothing was going to stop him.

* * *

When Worlds got back home, it was too quiet. He walked into the bedroom, and it looked like a tornado had hit. Clothes were thrown all over the place, and Dom lay in the bed sniffing from crying. Worlds walked over to where she was and pulled her

98

to the edge of the bed. He opened her legs, pulling her panties to the side, and began to finger her pussy. She wanted to object, but it felt too good. Her pussy was getting wetter and wetter by the second.

"Stop! I'm mad at you, nigga!" she moaned, spreading her legs wider for him.

He knew she didn't want him to stop, so he stuck another finger inside and then another, until he was fucking her with three fingers. He even stuck his thumb inside her ass, which caused her to cum instantly. That was only the beginning, as he started sucking on her clit. By this time, Dom wasn't even thinking about the argument they had earlier. She needed to feel him inside her.

"Oh, baby. I need some dick right now, please!" she begged, holding his head between her legs.

Worlds stood up, knowing that he had her where he wanted her. He took off his clothes and gave her what she needed for the next two hours. By the time he was done with her, she had fallen right to sleep, forgetting about everything that had happened.

Six

Beep! Beep! Beep! Beep!

The respirator machine that Riggs was hooked up to made a continuous sound.

He was in critical but stable condition after taking two bullets to the chest. The men who shot him thought he was dead because he lay still on the ground until they left. He thought at least his friend Fredd would help him, but he took off too. That left a sour taste in his mouth. However, he told himself that if the roles were reversed, he probably would have done the same thing.

Alexis stayed in the room with her man, not leaving his side except to use the bathroom or get something to eat. She wanted to go home and take a quick shower, but she didn't want to miss anything going on with his condition. They talked briefly the previous night, before the medicine knocked him right back out. She leaned her head back on the chair, trying to catch a quick nap, but was interrupted by the sound of the door opening. The doctor walked in with a clipboard in her hand.

"Hello! Are you awake?"

"Yes!" Alexis replied, standing up and stretching. "When will he be able to go home?"

"Well, that's the good news I came to give you. Everything looks normal," the doctor told her, looking at Riggs's chart. "His wounds are healing nicely, and there's no sign of infection. You can take him home today if you want."

Excitedly, Alexis nodded her head yes. Her man had been cooped up in that hospital too long. She needed to get him home where he could relax in the comfort of his own bed.

"Come with me so you can sign his release papers, and once he wakes up, you can take him home."

Alexis gave Riggs a kiss on the cheek before following the doctor to sign the discharge papers. She hoped he would be awake by the time she returned, or she was going to wake his ass up herself. She wanted to get out of there ASAP.

As if on cue, when Alexis returned, Riggs woke up with a groggy look on his face. He looked around the room like he was looking for something.

"Hey, baby, what's wrong?" she asked.

103

"Where are my clothes? I'm getting out of here before they try to keep me any longer."

"I just signed the papers, so you can come home now anyway, daddy. I got your clothes right here," she said, lifting up the shopping bag.

Thirty minutes later, they were in Alexis's car heading home. She made a few stops on the way, at Rite Aid and Pete's Steaks. She had to get his prescription filled and buy some bandages. They also got a couple of sandwiches because she didn't want to cook. When they got in the house, Riggs sat down on the couch.

"Did you hear anything from Fredd and Drew?" he asked, scrolling through his phone.

"Drew called several times checking up on you, but I only heard from Fredd the one time I told you

104

about. When I tried to call him back to let him know that you were okay, he never answered the phone. I would have left a message or texted him, but my only concern at the time was you."

"That's okay, momma. I'll hit him up in a few. Right now I need to talk to Drew," he said, pressing send on his iPhone.

He wanted to find out if niggas were talking about coming up on some work. His work! Whoever was behind his attempted murder and robbery was going to pay. Drew didn't answer, so he left a voice message. Riggs knew that once he saw the number, Drew would surely hit him right back.

His next call was to Fredd. After a couple of rings, Fredd picked up.

"Yo, who this?"

"This Riggs, my nigga! What's good?" he asked.

"Stop playing with me. My nigga Riggs got slumped by some bitch-ass nigga. So if you got his cell phone, when I find you, you're dead!" he said, making it seem like he was serious and unaware it was his friend.

Fredd knew it was Riggs. He had heard from one of his friends that he had survived the shooting. However, he didn't want to go visit him because he didn't know what to say. Eventually, he knew this call would be coming, so he wanted to see where Riggs's head was.

"This Riggs, man, I'm still breathing. They need to hit me more than twice for me to check. Why did you leave me like that for dead, bro? I wouldn't have left you."

"Man! Shit was crazy that day. I thought they were going to kill me too, but the gun jammed. If I would have known that you were still breathing, I would have helped you out. I heard the cop sirens and got out of there. I even looked for your gun since you're always strapped," he lied.

Riggs believed him, but there was just something about the way he said it that caused a little bit of doubt. "So, where you at now?"

"Down the bottom trying to get this money so I can get some work. Shit has been dry lately, man. Do you know where I can get something from?" Fredd asked.

Fredd had work already, but he didn't want Riggs to know that it was his work that was going around.

"I don't know yet. I have to see what's up with my cousin. He knows what happened to me, and I know he's still gonna want his money. Let me get back to you on that. Be safe out there, nigga. I'm about to eat with my girl."

"Okay, you too, bro! Just hit me up when you want me to swing past there."

"Cool! Did Worlds touch yet?"

"I don't know. I'll call his people and see what's good."

"Alright, cannon. See you later!" Riggs said, ending the call.

After calling his cousin and letting him know that he was out of the hospital, he and Alexis ate their food while watching a movie. Alexis wanted some dick, but she didn't want to hurt Riggs, so she just

108

gave him some head, and he played with her pussy until they both exploded. He promised that he would blow out her back in a couple of days when he was fully recovered. She couldn't wait either.

Seven

Worlds and Bubb made it to Philly just as rush hour was starting. Worlds only had one thing on his mind, and that was getting money. He wasn't broke, but he definitely wasn't comfortable either. He didn't even have his own car yet, so he depended on his girl or his niggas to take him everywhere. The bus was not an option because he was always strapped. Being without his gun was like being without his dick. People would think he was a pussy and try to stick him.

They pulled up on Mellon Street looking for Fredd. As they slowly drove down the block, niggas out hustling or playing craps looked up. They didn't recognize Bubb's car, so an alert went up. Were they cops or niggas trying to stick them? Worlds noticed the tension and placed his gun under his leg, just in chase shit got ugly. Bubb already had his .40 caliber out and had taken the safety off. He rolled down the window and showed that he came in peace.

"Yo, cannon! I'm just looking for my man Fredd. We was locked up together in Delaware County," Worlds said.

"Fredd ain't around here. That bitch-ass nigga up the street somewhere. Take y'all nut asses out of here before shit get crazy!" one of the young bulls said, lifting up his shirt and exposing his 9 mm.

Two of his goons did the same thing, trying to impress a couple of chicks standing beside them.

ERNEST MORRIS

"No doubt, bro!" Worlds said, signaling for Bubb to pull off.

"Yeah, roll the fuck up outta here, and don't come back," another one yelled. He threw a bottle, hitting Bubb's back window.

Bubb stopped abruptly and backed up his car. All the young boys standing out there suddenly stood up. If they only knew who they were fucking with, they would have scattered immediately. Bubb jumped out with an AR-15, and Worlds had a shottie, which he had had in the backseat.

"Move, and I'ma light this fucking block up like the Fourth of July!" Bubb yelled. "Which one of you bitch-ass niggas threw a bottle at my shit?"

112

None of them responded, so Worlds smacked the closest one to him in the face with the back of the gun, causing him to fall to the ground. Four of his teeth fell out along with some blood. One of the other lil niggas tried to pull out on them, but Bubb was on him.

Blaca! Blaca! Blaca!

He hit him with the assault rifle, instantly killing him. Nobody else dared to move. They put their hands in the air. One of them even pissed himself because he was so frightened.

"I'm only going to ask one more time, and then all of you are gonna lay the fuck down!" Bubb said, with murder in his eyes.

Fredd was turning the corner when he saw one of the young bulls drop dead from the shots. He was about to run the other way until he recognized one of the dudes.

"Yizzo, what's going on?" he asked as he was walking toward the group.

Worlds spun around ready to let go with the pump, until he saw who it was.

"These niggas are disrespectful and need to be taught a lesson," Bubb suggested.

"The police station is right up the street. Let's get out of here," Fredd said, hopping in the backseat of the car. "Come on, man! The cops are probably on their way."

Bubb and Worlds jumped into the car and peeled off as Fredd directed them to his crib on Reno Street.

Not trying to get caught, the young boys scattered down the street. They were happy that their lives had been spared for the moment.

"Nigga, when did you get home?" Fredd asked Worlds while giving him a pound.

"I've been out for a few. What's good though with the bull? Did you talk to him yet?" Worlds asked.

"I hit him a couple days ago, and he said everything was in place. He was just waiting for you."

Worlds figured he didn't want to deal with Fredd, which is why he told him that. He decided he would hit him up ASAP so he could make some money.

"How many blocks do you have out here so far?

I'm trying to flood all of them with some work."

"We got Mellon Street, but that block will be hot

for awhile now because of the body. I also have a

couple of blocks in the southwest that we can use.

These two young bulls from Delaware be trapping

out there. I just had a meeting with them about

copping from me. They can just trap for us," Fredd

told them.

"Okay! Well, I'm going to chill out this way for

tonight. I have to go see this chick that keeps hitting

my phone. She's about getting paper, so I'm gonna

put her on the team. I'm trying to hit up Vanity Grand

afterward so I can see what all this talk is about. You

rolling?" he asked Fredd.

"Hell yeah! Just hit my jack when you ready. I

also might have a couple more blocks. I'll let you

know about that tomorrow," Fredd stated, thinking

about South Philly.

"Those niggas still got my blood, dawg. I need to

relieve some tension, so I'll stay out here with you,"

Bubb said.

"Well, we'll get at you when we're ready to roll

out," Worlds said to Fredd as he and Bubb headed

out the door.

They shouldn't have stayed around that anyway

since they had just murked a nigga. They looked

around cautiously before jumping in the car and peeling off.

"I'm not going to show my face around there for awhile. Somebody might have said something," Bubb said as he headed out of North Philly.

Eight

Deja was sitting on the steps getting her hair braided from some shortie she met out in the Southwest. She needed her shit tight for when she and her crew hit the club later.

"So are you still gonna kick it with me tonight when you get back?" Neek asked.

"Definitely! If your sexy ass is still up when I get out of there," Deja replied, sticking her hand between Neek's legs and playing with her pussy.

Neek had to stop doing her hair for a minute because Deja had her pussy soaked, and she could feel her juices seeping through her panties.

"You have to stop that if you want me to finish your hair," Neek moaned, with her eyes closed.

Deja grew up in North Philly on 23rd and Diamond. She had been living out there most of her life. Growing up around five brothers made her tough as nails. She could hang with the toughest nigga around, blow for blow, and wouldn't back down. With all the toughness that she demonstrated, no one got to see the feminine side of her. Without a doubt, she was a dime piece.

She stood five five and weighed 130 pounds. She had a caramel complexion, a small waist with a fat ass, and D-cup breasts that she kept stuffed under her sports bra. When she wore some sexy clothes, no chick in Philly was fucking with her. She preferred to dress like a tomboy, though, and that still didn't hide the fact that she was bad. She was bisexual, though, so both men and women had their chance with her.

"Okay! I'ma chill out so you can finish. I'm tearing that ass up later, though."

Neek just smiled and finished doing her braids.

When she got close to being done, Deja stood up to stretch. She turned to say something to Neek, when she felt cold steel against the back of her head.

"You know what it is. Give that shit up or lay down!" the voice said.

Deja didn't even flinch, but Neek was scared as hell. Deja just shook her head no.

"I'm not giving up shit, so do what you gotta do!" Deja replied.

Worlds laughed as he took the gun from her head and tucked it under his shirt.

"I caught your ass slipping, didn't I?"

"Not really, cannon," she said, looking down toward his dick. "I'm always on point."

Worlds looked down and noticed the .25 aimed at his shit. He shook his head in disbelief at how on point she was. They gave each other a hug as Bubb stepped out of the car. Worlds then introduced them to each other, and they gave a head nod to one another.

"I told you niggas ain't fucking with her," Worlds bragged to Bubb.

"She's the real deal!" he smiled.

"But anyway, Deja, I need to holla at you on some real shit!" Worlds said, with a more serious look on his face.

"What's up?"

"I want you to get down with us on some get-messy shit. I know you do your boosting thing, but I need someone like you to run North Philly for me. All you have to do is collect the money and make sure nothing comes back short. If you need a gun or manpower, just give me a call."

Deja stood there for a minute to take it all in. She had never sold drugs before, and as tempting as his offer was now, she needed more time to think about it before making her decision.

"Let me give it some thought for a day or two, Worlds. You know I'm more into other shit than that, but I will give you an answer. Right now, though, I'm trying to get ready for the club," she stated, rubbing her hands together. "What you niggas getting into tonight?"

"We going to Vanity Grand. Which one are you going to?"

"The same place. Y'all trying to roll deep with me and my girls, or what? We won't cock block you!" she told him, giving him a nudge with her elbow.

"We can do that, baby girl! Just make sure you dress to impress. Of course, we are," Worlds replied, heading for the car.

"Don't worry. We will be."

When they got back on the road, Worlds decided it was time to give bull a call and set things in motion. By this time next week, he was hoping to have more dope than anybody else around.

* * *

Vanity Grand was packed by the time Worlds, Bubb, Deja, and the rest of her lil crew arrived. Worlds and Bubb pulled up in a rented 2017 Audi 8, and Deja and three other girls were in a 2017 Acura RL. The car actually belonged to one of the girl's brothers, who was getting at a couple of dollars. He purchased it from a chop shop out in the Northeast.

Worlds had on a fresh pair of Butters, True Religion jeans, and a fitted T-shirt that made him look cut up. Bubb had on similar attire; the only difference was that he rocked all-black everything. He stayed on his grimy shit just in case muthafuckas got out of pocket.

Deja stepped out of the car in a Chanel dress that came just above the knee, and a pair of five-inch stilettos that wrapped around her leg up to her thighs.

Her individual braids flowed down her back. She had on costume jewelry that looked so real that it sparkled from the light.

Her friend Dyhria wore a strapless Christian Dior pencil dress and four-inch stilettos. She had long, straight hair that came almost to her ass, because of her heritage. She was Egyptian and Puerto Rican and had emerald eyes. She stood five seven and weighed 120 pounds. She had perky C-cup breasts and a nicely proportioned ass that made her figure perfect.

Carmela had a caramel complexion and juicy lips. She had on a low-cut black dress with the back out. It was so short that if she moved the wrong way, her whole ass would be exposed. She had on three-inch red pumps, with a matching purse. She was biracial as well, a mixture of Black and Jamaican.

Last but not least was Melody, who was the thickest of the crew. She stood five four and weighed 142 pounds. She had DD breasts and short hair. Melody had on a pair of Apple Bottoms jeans with a tight fitted shirt, letting everyone know she had big perky titties underneath. She never sported a bra, and they still sat straight up. She wore thigh-high boots, with the jeans tucked inside of them.

All the women were indeed dressed to impress. They had niggas gawking with their eyes as they all headed to the VIP section. The server brought over two complimentary bottles to the group.

"The owner says these are on the house," she told them, setting the bottles on the table. She looked at the group of women and gave them a seductive smile before glancing at Worlds. "He would like to talk to you in his office for a minute."

Worlds didn't even know the owner, so he wondered what this was about. Curiously he got up and followed her upstairs, through a couple of doors, and into the office, where two men were talking while looking out at the crowd. Once the server stepped out and closed the door behind her, they introduced themselves.

"Hello, Donte!" one man said, calling him by his real name. "My name is Evani, and this is Carlos."

They both shook Worlds's hand before inviting him to sit down. Wanting to get down to business so he could get back to the fun downstairs with his friends, Worlds said, "So, what did you need to see me for, and thanks for the bottles."

128

"You're welcome, chico. And it seems that we have a mutual friend," Evani began. "You talked to my father's partner earlier about getting some work on consignment."

Worlds only talked to one person earlier, and it was only briefly because they didn't want to discuss anything over the phone. He wondered how the hell they knew that.

Evani then saw the look of confusion on Worlds's face and decided to calm his suspicions.

"No, we are not cops, feds, or any other law enforcement agency. My dad's name is Santiago, and his partner is E.J. He called me earlier today and told me you would be coming here tonight. That's why you and your friends are getting the red carpet treatment."

"Wait! So E.J. told you to hook us up?" Worlds asked, not really believing him.

"Yes, he and my father are in Florida. I control everything on this side for them. If you don't believe me, I can put you on speaker phone right now," Evani stated, holding the phone handset up for Worlds.

At that moment, Worlds realized just how big E.J. really was. He had ties to the Mexican cartel. Worlds felt like he had just cashed in on something big.

"That won't be necessary," Worlds replied, with a slight grin on his face, thinking about dollar signs.

"Okay, well I know you want to finish enjoying yourself, so this is for you," Carlos spoke up and said, passing him a cell phone. "Something will be arriving at your girlfriend Dominique's house in the morning, or would you like it to go to your baby mom Amanda's house?"

Worlds looked up in surprise when Carlos said Dom's and Amanda's names. They knew more about him than he did about them. He just shook his head.

"Dom's house is cool. I'll be there waiting when it arrives. But what time will it be there?" he questioned.

"Around noon. Is that okay?" Carlos asked.

"Yeah, that is cool."

"Okay! Well it will be two keys of pure heroin. The going price for it is $75,000 a key. Since we are giving it to you on consignment, that price stands. How fast will you be able to move that kind of work?" Evani asked.

"I, or should I say we, can start as soon as we get it. I don't see it being a problem. I have a good team that I just put together. Me and my partner, Fredd, will have Philly and Chester popping in no time."

"Okay, great! We will only deal with you, though, not your friend. You should be careful around him too," Carlos warned.

Worlds brushed it off, not even thinking about what they just said about Fredd. He was just glad to finally have a connect. The men talked for about ten more minutes before Worlds went back down to the VIP section with his friends. Tomorrow would be the start of business, but tonight was his time to have fun.

* * *

Fredd arrived at the club an hour late. He told Worlds he would meet him there, because he had something to do.

He and Terrance were staking out a spot owned by a couple of bikers. Someone told him they were sitting on major paper and also drugs. Fredd wanted it all, so they had been watching them for a week. They wanted to wait for about a month before going in. That way they would have their whole routine down pat.

After getting frisked by the bouncers, Fredd and Terrance made their way over to the VIP section where Worlds, Bubb, and the girls were drinking and enjoying the strippers.

"What's up, nigga?" Fredd said, greeting Worlds with a half hug.

After everyone was introduced, Fredd poured himself a drink.

"Yo! Everything is a go on that situation," Worlds whispered to Fredd as a thick white girl gave him a lap dance.

"That's what's up, so when will we be set?"

"Tomorrow."

"Okay. What's up with these shorties you with?" he asked, staring at Deja and her crew.

"They're off limits, bro. They are a part of the team," Worlds told him.

Fredd just nodded his head but kept staring at one girl in particular. Carmela's ass was bouncing as she danced to the music. His dick got hard just from staring at the thong that was swallowed up by her cheeks. The strippers were there for the night, courtesy of Carlos and Evani, but all he wanted was her.

"We'll be back. We're going over to the stage to make it rain on these bitches," Deja said to Worlds, leading her friends out of the VIP area.

"So what's really the deal with you and Deja?" Bubb said, trying to get the scoop.

"Nothing. I helped her out of a jam awhile ago. She almost got pickled trying to steal at the Macy's at King of Prussia Mall, and I got her up out of there."

"Damn! You saved her ass. So now she's been loyal to you. So what will they be doing?" Bubb asked.

"Working!" Worlds said, giving Bubb a crazy look. "This ain't no free ride for anybody. We all got to do our parts."

"Well, if you need me, bro, you know where—" Bubb couldn't finish his sentence because he noticed

135

some shit about to pop off by the stage. "Why that nigga keep trying to grab homegirl?"

Worlds looked over toward the stage to see some dude smack the shit out of Carmela. Before he could stand all the way up, Deja dropped the nigga with a bottle to the back of his head. She and the other girls started stomping him on the ground. A few of his boys started rushing over toward them.

"Let's go!" Worlds said, rushing through the crowd, with Bubb and Fredd on his heels.

One dude tried to swing but was quickly put on his ass with a hang maker from Bubb. Worlds gripped one of the other niggas by the collar, pulling down his face and then kneeing him in the mouth. Blood flowed everywhere. People in the crowd watched the fight in awe, until about fifteen bouncers rushed in, grabbing the niggas and tossing them out.

Worlds and Deja helped Carmela to the ladies' room

to fix herself up. Worlds stayed by the door until they

came out. Even though they didn't have to leave,

they wanted to get the fuck up outta there.

"We're going to head home so I can make sure

that she gets in the house safe. Are you staying out

this way tonight or going back out to Chester?" Deja

asked Worlds.

"I have some shit to take care of, so I'm going

home. Are you good?"

"Yeah, I'm good!" she replied, lifting up her

dress a little to show him her gun that was strapped

to her leg.

"I don't even know why I asked," Worlds said, shutting the door after she got in. "Y'all ladies take care, and I'll hit your jack tomorrow."

"Okay! And I'm with you on that thing we talked about too. Me and my girls can handle shit out there."

"Say no more!" he said, watching as the ladies pulled off.

He rushed over to the car so he could get home as quickly as possible. He knew that Dom was going to flip out. She didn't even call to see where he was at. That right there told him that he was in trouble.

Nine

The four hundred bundles that Zy and Torey had copped from Fredd went in no time. They needed more because the fiends loved that shit. It was around ten o'clock in the morning when they met up with Fredd at the Sunoco on 52nd & Spruce. Fredd and Terrance pulled into the station a couple minutes later and parked on the side right next to them. Fredd got out and jumped into the backseat of their car.

"What's good with you, nigga?" Torey said, giving him a nod.

"Shit! You know me, just trying to get this money. My man is meeting up with our plug right now, so I will have something ready for y'all by tonight."

"I thought you had something for us now. We could have waited 'til later," Zy replied, with frustration.

"Yeah, Fredd, we told muthafuckas we would be back up within an hour. Now they might try to cop from someone else," Torey added.

"I have something to hold you off for now if you want it?" he replied. "Or you can get in on this lick that me and my man's about to handle today."

"What you talking about?" Zy asked, interested.

"We've been watching this spot for awhile now, and these niggas is getting money. I'm trying to hit them today while they still have everything there. It's only a couple of them there in the morning, so we can be in and out."

"Why you want to hit these niggas in broad daylight? That shit is too risky. What if people see us and call the cops?" Torey asked.

"Trust me! Ain't nobody gonna be around this place, and they sure as hell not calling no pigs. Two of my homies are out there now waiting for us. So are y'all in or out?"

Both Zy and Torey looked at each other momentarily, thinking about the situation. The look in their eyes said it all without even speaking. If this nigga tried some funny shit, they were going to lay his ass down, and whoever was with him. They wanted that bread, so they agreed to go with them.

"Follow us to the spot so we can go over the plan and load up. We have heat, so y'all don't have to use your own shit!" Fredd said, stepping out of the car.

"We good on that part. I only use my shit! That way there are no problems," Zy told him.

"Suit yourself! Let's get this money!"

Fredd walked back over to the car and hopped in with Terrance. He gave him a head nod, which indicated that the two men were in. Terrance smiled and pulled off, with Zy and Torey following.

* * *

When Worlds had returned home last night, Dom wasn't even there. He walked into the bedroom and noticed that most of her stuff was gone. He figured she was tired of his shit and left him. He didn't care, because all that was on his mind was getting back up. As he sat on the edge of his bed in a wifebeater and boxers, he thought about what kind of money they would be bringing in off of the work, and a smile crept across his face. His thoughts were interrupted by a knock on the door.

Worlds quickly threw on a pair of shorts and then headed downstairs. When he looked through the peephole, a guy was standing there in a FedEx uniform. Thinking that it was a package for Dom, Worlds opened the door.

"What's up, man?"

"Good morning, sir! I just need you to sign right here, please," the delivery man said, passing him the tablet. Worlds quickly signed and then took the package from him. When he looked down at the name on the address, he looked back up at the man.

"I didn't order shit!"

"Mr. Evani said that he will contact you later and that you will be pleased with the contents," the man said before walking away, getting inside the van, and pulling away.

Worlds already knew what it was, and a smile grew on his face. It was time to get paid. He opened the box, and the first thing he saw was a cell phone. He removed it, along with the plastic that was concealing something at the bottom. He pulled out three packages and set them on the table. He was only expecting two, so when he saw the third one, he realized what the delivery man meant.

He called Bubb to come pick him up so they could get to Philly to start bagging up. That's why he needed Deja's friends. She would be in charge of that

part. After he hung up with Bubb, he called Deja to

inform her that he would be there in an hour and a

half. He got dressed and ate a bowl of cereal before

Bubb arrived.

* * *

Two hours later, they were sitting in Deja's

kitchen. Worlds removed one of the packages from

the book bag he was carrying and set it on the table.

Bubb and Deja pulled up two chairs and sat next to

him, to get a better look at the work. Worlds pulled

out his pocket knife and dug into a corner of the brick

to open it up. The three of them looked at the brown

block and frowned up their faces in a puzzled look.

They had no idea that heroin was brown like that. It was so brown that it almost looked like chocolate.

But Worlds remembered Evani and Carlos saying that he would be getting raw dope, but that was an understatement. That shit was almost pure. Worlds knew he could probably cut it seven times, but he was only going to do it five times. That way they would more than triple their money and wouldn't kill friends in the process. People would surely leave the other dealers alone and only fuck with them once they tasted it.

"This shit is crazy!" Deja said, looking at the brick. "What do you need me to do?"

"Have your girls come over and help cut, bag, and stamp everything up. That's what you're in charge of. You can also drop off when the corners get low, or have one of them do it. Is that cool with you?" Worlds asked.

"Hell yeah! They are upstairs chilling right now. I'm gonna call them so we can get started," Deja replied, heading for the stairs.

"Deja!" Worlds yelled, stopping her before she reached the top of the steps. "They have to wear masks and gloves. And the only clothes they can have on is their panties. I don't want no one trying to take my shit. Is that cool?"

"For that money, these bitches will walk around this muthafucka butt naked and twerking their asses in the process," she replied, smiling at Worlds.

"Well! Go get them so I can show them how I want it done. Then we're gonna set up shop and get paid."

"This shit is going to have niggas on their backs," Bubb stated, looking at the brown brick.

"That's the idea, bro. So start opening that up while I get the bags and shit ready and call Fredd."

Worlds wanted to move the work a little differently. They would sell it by the gram or the bundle. The grams would go for $60, as would the bundles. A smart person would buy the gram, and they could get almost two-and-a-half bundles, but that would be unlikely. People were so anxious and in a rush to get high, and blinded by reality, that they were only getting fourteen bags in a bundle for sixty

148

dollars and didn't even see the benefit in buying a gram. It didn't really matter to Worlds how they got it, though, as long as the money was coming in.

He spent the next two hours showing the girls how to bag and stamp the heroin. He even showed them just how much cut to put on it, using the fentanyl so they didn't fuck the money up. After the first hour, you would have thought they had been doing it all their lives. They had it down to a science, and Worlds enjoyed the fact that he could go handle other things while they were doing that.

"Deja, me and Bubb got some shit to take care of. If you need me, just hit my jack."

"Cool! You gonna drop these packs off, or you want me to do it?" she asked, watching the girls handle the work.

"I'll take what you got now, but after that, you handle all of it. I have to see for myself what the blocks are going to do at first anyway."

He stashed the work into the book bag as he and Bubb hit the streets. He tried calling Fredd again but got no answer.

Where the fuck is this nigga at? he thought to himself as they headed to Chester to get it poppin'.

* * *

"Okay! Everybody know what to do, right?" Fredd said, looking in the back of the stolen van.

Everyone responded with a head nod except for Chubb, who didn't like the fact that Fredd was trying to act like the boss.

Fredd just ignored him as he cocked the riot pump he was holding. A series of guns cocking followed as they all then pulled their masks down over their faces.

"Let's do it!" Zy said impatiently.

They all hopped out, running into the club. As soon as people saw the men rush in, they all got scared and put their hands in the air.

"Anybody move, they die!" Fredd said as the six men surrounded the people at the bar and card games.

The men at the table looked at the group of masked men to see what they wanted.

Fredd walked up to the man sitting there like he was in charge, and aimed the pump at his face. He demanded the money and drugs that he knew were there.

"Do you have any idea who you're robbing?" the man said, without an ounce of fear in his voice.

"You think I give a damn?" Fredd said as he smacked him with the butt of the gun. "Now shut the fuck up!"

The man bent over, holding the back of his head. When he looked up at Fredd, he stared right into his eyes without even blinking and said, "You better sleep with one eye open, nigga! That's not a threat either, so do what you got to," he said, knowing they were black from the way they talked.

Tired of listening to the man, Chubb walked over

and pushed Fredd out of the way. He gripped the man by the collar and picked him up out of the chair.

"Where is the stash at, old man, and you and everybody else get to walk up out of here!"

"Fuck you!" the man replied.

Chubb let him go and then turned around like he was about to walk away. However, he then spun back around so quickly that nobody saw it coming.

Boc!

One shot from the calico tore into his kneecap and shattered the bone, separating the connecting joints. The pain the bullet inflicted made him obey their command. If he wasn't convinced before, he was now. These niggas weren't playing games.

"It's in the back room!" he screamed out in pain.

Zy and Robert Sean searched through the back room vigorously until they found the money and work. It was nowhere near what they were expecting to find. After bagging everything up, they came back out with everything in hand.

"Let's get the fuck out of here!" Zy announced, heading for the door.

The group of masked men started backing toward the door, never taking their eyes off of the men in the bar. Once everyone was in the van, Chubb just had to do something extra. He turned around and let off numerous shots into the building, not caring if he hit anyone. He then hopped into the van. They fled away from the scene thinking they were in the clear.

"What the fuck was that shit you just did? We were just supposed to grab the shit and get out!" Fredd said angrily, mean-mugging Chubb.

"I got answers, and because of it, this is what we got!" Chubb replied, pointing to the bag of dope and money. "He wasn't telling your bitch ass anything!"

Fredd was tired of Chubb disrespecting him every time his mouth opened. He wanted to put a bullet right through his skull. Feeling the tension in the air, Torey tried to ease it up. "So how much you niggas think was in there?"

"It wasn't as much as we thought it would be, but they did have some gwap for us. I'm trying to figure out what kind of drugs this is, though," Zy said, digging into the bag and pulling out a package with the substance in it.

"We'll figure shit out when we get back to the crib. Put that up for now," Fredd said, looking at the missed calls on his phone.

He redialed Worlds's number so he could talk to him. If they only knew what was about to come their way, they would have killed everybody in that place.

Ten

Detective Campbell sat at his desk looking over some pictures of a crime scene. It was puzzling to him because of what the witness said she saw. He knew she wasn't telling him everything she knew, but he didn't want to interrogate her too much yet. He was also waiting for his partner to get back with the video surveillance tapes from the store up the street where the murders took place.

As if on cue, Detective Henson walked right in and sat down across from him at her desk. She held up the DVD and had a smile on her face. "Our witness has been lying to us about what she saw, and I got the proof right here!"

ERNEST MORRIS

"Talk to me!" Campbell said, giving her his full attention.

He was hoping that they were about to crack this case wide open.

"Well, not only does she know the shooters; she knows the male victim as well. The tape shows her and the female victim standing outside the bodega talking to the male. Her friend passed him what looks to be a house key, and he walks off in one direction, while they head back in the other direction," she said, pausing so Campbell could take in what had she said so far.

"About half an hour later, the two girls returned to the same corner, but this time they hoped inside of a Pontiac Grand Prix with tinted windows. It doesn't

158

show who was inside, but I'm willing to bet a hundred dollars that it's the killer or killers."

Detective Campbell rubbed his beard as he listened to his partner. What they had was hopefully just enough to finally get the girl to tell them what really had happened in the house that night.

"So what do you think? It was a robbery gone bad, and she and her friend had something to do with it?" Campbell asked.

"Yep! But it went bad for them, because whoever they tried to rob was ready for the ambush!" Detective Henson replied.

"Okay! Let's watch the DVD so I can hopefully catch something that you missed. Then we're gonna go pay our witness another visit. This time, though, we won't be so nice!" Campbell said as they got up and headed to the video room.

"Uh oh! I know that look! What do you have up your sleeve, Tony?" she said to her partner, giving him a look of suspicion.

"I'll tell you all about it after we finish watching the video. I just have to make sure I'm not wrong on this first," he stated, closing the door behind them.

They sat in the video room and played the surveillance video over and over again for the next hour, trying to find something helpful to the case. Once they finished, they decided to talk to Nydiyah first thing in the morning. They then headed home for the night.

* * *

It hadn't been a full two months yet, and already Worlds and Fredd had made their mark in the streets as the new top dogs. There wasn't an ounce, quarter, half, or whole brick of heroin sold in Philly, Chester, Delaware, or Jersey that they didn't have a part in. It was amazing to them, almost unbelievable, the amount of money they saw and drugs they sold in the past month and a half.

Being on top wasn't as easy as it seemed. There were more than enough problems that came along with the job. Workers were being busted and fucking up with money. Some claimed to be stuck up. You name it, it happened. It was definitely a hassle. In fact, it was a headache for them, but at the end of the day, it was all worth it. Whatever the case was, the streets were theirs now, or so they thought.

Fredd was still running around, recklessly robbing people, without Worlds even knowing. He wanted it all, and nothing was going to stop him. Little did he know that Terrance and the others even robbed their people a couple of times but didn't say anything to Fredd. They kept the work and money for themselves.

Zy and Torey had joined up with Worlds and Fredd, and their blocks were back to doing numbers. Worlds sold them a brick a week, and the money was coming in. As long as Worlds dealt with Evani and Carlos, he figured he would be a millionaire within the next year.

Deja went from having just her three friends cutting, bagging, and stamping the dope to hiring six more women to help. They even expanded to a house on 2nd and Lehigh. Niggas thought she was sweet until she laid a couple of them down for trying her. They quickly realized that she was that bitch. Worlds was proud that he put the right person in charge of the stash houses.

Worlds and Fredd headed over to the house because he wanted to meet up with the top people. Even though Deja wasn't a partner, he considered her one. Fredd had something that he needed to do, so he was hoping that it wouldn't take long. He had another meeting to be at with some people about some work he didn't know what to do with.

They pulled up to the crib, looking around and making sure nothing seemed out of place. They had to be that way because niggas would do anything to be in their positions. They would never catch them slipping, though.

They stepped out of the car and entered the building. When they walked into the apartment that was used as the conference room, twenty-two people were sitting around the table waiting. Deja was one of them. Fredd and Worlds stood at the head of the table so they could start the meeting.

"Okay, this is how it is. We have a sweet connect for the dope in Florida as well as in Mexico. They will get it to us in a timely fashion, and it's our job to get rid of it. The faster we can get rid of it, the faster we get more. I'm trying to lock up the East Coast.

Deja will take care of the distribution to all the North

Philly houses like she has been, and Fredd will

handle West Philly. I will handle Chester. We have

twenty-one houses now. That means the twenty-one

of you sitting here are the heads of the households.

Anything goes wrong, you need to call one of us

immediately. Got it?" Worlds said as everyone

nodded their heads.

"I just got us a few people on payroll from police

stations in all our areas who will keep us in the loop

on any investigations or random raids. It's pretty

simple, so we all have to do our parts," Fredd

explained as he rubbed his hands together.

Just as Worlds was about to say something else, the front door opened. Everyone looked in that direction and stared at the figure standing before them. You would have thought they had seen a ghost. No one in their right mind expected to see this person, not even Worlds or Fredd. He walked toward the table accompanied by the most beautiful woman they had ever seen. Even Deja's pussy tingled at the sight of her.

At twenty-six years of age, Yahnise was a bombshell. She stood five six, and her slender build gave her the look of a model, as did her facial features. Her neck was slim, long, and very delicate looking, and her shoulders dropped just right. Her face was oval and very much chiseled to perfection.

Everything from her strapless Chanel dress to her three-inch stilettos screamed money. There was nobody fucking with her, and she knew it.

"What kind of operation are you running where people can just walk through the front door? Where is security? Better yet, why isn't anyone guarding the front door? Where are the shooters that should have been posted on the roof guarding your money?" he inquired with a calm yet attention-demanding voice.

No one could speak because they were still in awe of the man talking to them.

"What's wrong? Y'all act like y'all seen a ghost!"

One of the young bulls at the table spoke up.

"I thought you were dead, sir. I went to your funeral with my mom!" he explained as everyone else at the table nodded in agreement.

They all had been in their teens when they went to the biggest homecoming of a street legend. E.J.'s funeral was so packed that the police had to block off seven blocks all around the church. People from all over came to say their goodbyes to the person who was now standing before them.

"The funeral was an illusion to trick everybody and keep me safe from the feds as well as my enemies. It's amazing how many people looked into the casket but never checked to see if the person inside was breathing!" E.J. stated. "I'm not here to talk about that right now, though. I'm here checking on my investment, and I'm not liking what I see. I want to speak with Worlds, so everybody else get out!"

They all looked from E.J. to Worlds, but no one moved. E.J. removed his glasses from his face, and the murderous look in his eyes said it all.

"Now!" he yelled.

Everyone jumped up and headed out the door, never looking back. Yahnise put her hand on his arm and whispered in his ear.

"I'll be outside in the car. Don't be too long, because we have to be on our jet to Mexico in two hours," she reminded him before giving him a kiss on the cheek and walking out the door so the men could talk.

As Fredd and Deja headed outside, the whole block was surrounded by men dressed all in black, carrying assault rifles. That's when Fredd really realized how powerful his friend from prison truly was. He was a little mad that he only wanted to talk to Worlds, but he didn't care, because he had to get somewhere important.

"What was that all about?" Deja asked Fredd as they stood outside the door, staring at the men in black.

"I'm not even sure, but whatever happened, it made my homie come all the way from MIA to address it. I have to go handle something, but tighten up security around here. Get a couple of shooters up on each roof so nothing like this will happen again," Fredd said as he headed for his car.

"What if Worlds needs to talk to you?" Deja said, watching Yahnise walk to the awaiting car parked in the middle of the street.

"Tell him to hit my phone. I'll be back in a couple of hours to check on you," he stated before hopping into the car and pulling off.

* * *

"So what brings you all the way out here?" Worlds asked, giving E.J. a half hug.

"I came to pick up my wife's cousin. She missed her, so you know how that is. I could have easily put her ass on a plane, but I also wanted to check on

171

Carlos and Evani. I see that business is booming right now," he said, sitting on the edge of the table.

"Yeah! We have a lot of area on lock right now. I'm trying to have this shit the way you had it!" Worlds said.

"No! I want you to just do you, and you will prosper in this game."

"So why did you need to talk to me alone?"

E.J. stood up and paced back and forth around the room a couple of times before stepping in front of Worlds.

"I want you to take a good look at your inner circle and make sure that everyone is in their right spot on your team. Fredd's supposed to be your partner, but there's something about him that's not

172

adding up. You can tell a man's heart by his eyes. The eyes never lie, Worlds. That is why I'm only dealing with you. Just be careful with the company you keep!"

Worlds listened to E.J. talk for a while. He thought about what he had told him, because it was the second time someone had said that to him. This time, though, he would be hands-on with everything going on.

"Thanks for coming, though, and I'm going to tighten up on things to make sure this operation is running smooth," Worlds stated.

"Well, let me get out of here. If you need to speak with me, just let Evani or Carlos know, and either one of them will be able to contact me. I can't keep the misses waiting too long." He smirked, shaking

Worlds's hand.

Worlds watched as E.J. left the building. E.J.'s

henchmen waited until he was safely in the SUV

before they dispersed into one of the six other SUVs.

The fleet of cars pulled out into traffic like they

owned the city. Worlds knew he would be that way

one day, and he smiled at his homie.

Eleven

Over the next couple of weeks, Riggs lay low, letting the healing process of his body take place. Every day he talked to Drew, who kept his ears in the streets to see if he heard anything yet, but still no luck. He was starting to get impatient, because the longer he sat around, the longer he wouldn't make any money. It was time to start getting some answers to the questions he had on his mind.

He strapped on his shoulder holster along with his twin Glocks, after putting on his bulletproof vest. He then slid the extra clips in place. He walked over to the mirror to check himself out. Riggs had on all black, with a skully cap to match. After being satisfied with his appearance, he went downstairs to wait for Drew, who was on his way over to pick him up.

***

"What's up with you? You ready to go put in some work?" Drew asked when Riggs got into the car.

"I was born ready! Now let's go find out where my shit at!" Riggs replied as he leaned back in the seat.

"This dude's mom who I know from the southeast asked me if I had put out some work there, because she's seen the bags with the same stamp that we use, about two weeks ago when she copped something. When I asked her where, she said over on

Woodland Avenue, so I think we should start there,"

Drew stated.

"The dumb muthafuckas didn't even change the

bags! How stupid can they be? Let's head over there

and pay these niggas a little visit!" Riggs said,

puffing on some loud. "They should have never

taken my shit!"

* * *

"What you need, Mike?" Lil Rel asked as the

fiend walked over toward the group of boys.

"Let me get two Bs," Mike replied, holding up

the money for them.

"Give me the dough and walk over to my man.

He will take care of you," Lil Rel stated. "I need

some more of that loud that Zy gave us that time. That shit was fine!"

"I know, man! I haven't had anything like that in a minute. When he comes to pick this money up, I'ma ask him where I can get some more of it all," Ant said.

"Yeah! I can smoke half a Dutch and be lit off that shit. We definitely need that. I'll pay him for a g.p. of it."

"Me too! We can grab that and blow it with these two freaks out north this weekend. They both keep blowing up my phone trying to hook up again. I told them MOB."

"Money over bitches!" they both said in unison.

"Yo! Who that cruising through the block like that?" Rel asked, watching the Ford Taurus slow down a little.

The windows were tinted, so they couldn't see inside.

"It's probably the pigs. I'm glad we don't have anything on us right now. You sold the last joints you had, right?" Ant asked.

"Yeah! That's why I told bull to get it from you. I'm about to get the rest out of the crib when these muthafuckas leave and stop harassing us."

The car kept going, not even paying them any attention. They watched it turn the corner, and then they smiled at each other. There were a few people outside, so they thought that the cops didn't feel like hearing the people's mouths.

"They must have thought we were going to run or something. We sure showed their asses!" Ant said, with a laugh.

* * *

"Why didn't you stop? That's them pussies right there!" Riggs said impatiently.

"Man! It's too many people outside right now, bro. We can wait and come back later to get them," Drew replied.

"Fuck those people! Go back around the block, nigga! We gonna set an example out of this bitch. Nobody takes my shit and thinks I'm just gonna let it slide. I bet no one will disrespect us again. I'm going

180

to get some answers right now, even if I have to expose these bitch-ass niggas in front of everybody. Now stop right in front of them!" Riggs demanded.

Thinking erratically, Riggs jumped out of the car, with his hand gripping the Glock that he pulled out from its holster. The move he made was so sudden that it caught everyone on the block by surprise.

"Listen up!" he began as he waved the gun aimlessly at the crowd of people, who were scrambling to get out of the way. "I want every last one of you lil niggas to pay attention 'cause I'm dead fucking serious!"

Riggs spoke to no one in particular because he didn't know who knew something about his shit, but he still continued to yell at the niggas, who were left frozen in their tracks.

Ant and Rel stood there stuck, wishing they had gone inside the house like they had started. They didn't even have their guns, which were hiding under the front tires of their cars parked in front of the door. When Riggs walked over toward them and singled them out, they knew something was about to happen.

"You two bitch-ass niggas, come the fuck over here! I believe y'all have or had something that belongs to me, and I want it back. I also want to know who gave it to you!" he said, not wanting to play games.

"Nigga! We don't know what the fuck you talking about, so miss me with that shit you talking!"

Rel stated, not backing down from the two men holding the guns on them.

When Rel puffed out his chest like he wanted to fight or something, Riggs lifted the Glock and aimed it at his leg.

Boc! Boc!

The gun sounded, and Rel screamed like a bitch getting beaten the fuck up.

"Shut your bitch ass up, nigga, before the next shot rocks your ass to sleep!" he snapped.

The people from the block watching were scared to death and didn't know what to do. Rel held his leg, while Ant stood there motionless.

"I want to know who came up with the bright idea to rob me and try to kill me?" he said, looking over at Ant for an answer.

"Like my man said, we don't know what the fuck you're talking about. We got our work from my man, and even if I did know, I wouldn't tell you shit. I'm no snitch, muthafucka!" Ant yelled back.

Riggs liked the young bull's heart, but right now he wasn't trying to hear any of that. He walked up to Ant and smacked him in the head with his gun.

"Both of you get in the trunk right now before you don't see tomorrow."

When neither of them moved, Drew took over and shot Rel in his other knee.

Boc!

"Okay, okay, nigga! Don't shoot him again," Ant yelled out, feeling sorry for his friend.

Drew popped open the trunk of the car, and Ant helped his homie over to the car. He hoped that someone had called the police and informed them of the shots. He didn't like the cops, but they were the only ones who might be able to save them right now. Once they both were in the trunk, Drew got in the driver's seat, while Rigs addressed the crowd of onlookers that was still left.

"If I find out any of you called the cops, that will be you taking that ride next!" Riggs said as he hopped in the car and Drew sped off.

A few minutes later, cops were everywhere trying to figure out what was going on.

* * *

They had the two young boys tied up in an

185

abandoned building by a junkyard on 61st and Passyunk Avenue. Since all the junkyards were closed, they weren't worried about anyone hearing them. Riggs stood over Rel, who was still in so much pain.

"I see you're not talking all that shit now, are you?" Riggs smirked. "I just want to know where my work and money are, and I'll let you walk, I mean crawl, up outta here!"

Rel looked up, ice-grilling Riggs and Drew. If looks could kill, they both would have been dead. Riggs walked over to Ant, who until now hadn't been touched.

"Are you gonna tell us what we need to know, or do you want the same thing we gave your friend over

186

there?"

"Fuck you! I'm not telling you shit!" Ant
exclaimed before spitting in Riggs's face.

Riggs wiped his face with the bottom part of his
shirt. He nodded over to Drew, who had a bat resting
on his shoulder. Drew smiled and walked up to Ant
and started swinging wildly at his body. He
continuously hit him with the wooden bat. Ant
caught a barrage of painful blows, mostly to his arms
and legs. Once he became tired of swinging the bat,
Drew then began punching Ant repeatedly in the
face.

Ant was covered in blood by the time Drew took
a break from the vicious attack. There was an
enormous amount of pain shooting throughout his

entire body. He laughed maniacally to further infuriate them. Riggs and Drew beat Ant over and over again for twenty minutes straight. They were violent and callous in their attempt to get answers, but he held water. Anyone else in his situation would have broken, but not Ant. Unhappy about his obvious lack of willingness to cooperate, Riggs shot him in the head at point-blank range.

Rel was struggling to get free, when he saw his man take a bullet to the head. He knew he had to do something if he wanted to get out of this alive. They approached him, ready to end his life as well, when he nodded his head in defeat.

Drew removed the duct tape from Rel's mouth. "You want to tell us something?" he questioned.

"I'll tell you where we got the work from. Just, please, don't kill me!" Rel said, defeated.

"Who gave it to you?" Riggs asked in a calm voice.

Rel started telling everything he knew in an attempt to live. He really didn't know anything, but he gave them all types of information, like he was talking to the cops. If he only knew how close to the truth he really was, he might have said something earlier. Riggs and Drew listened to Rel talk, with anger all over their faces. Riggs couldn't believe the name that came out of his mouth.

After they got what they needed from Rel, Drew silenced him forever with two shots to the heart. Usually he would have given him a wig shot, but because he told them what they needed to know, they let his family be able to give him an open-casket funeral instead of a closed one. They left the two bodies there to be found by whoever opened the building in the morning, as they headed back home to prepare for war.

* * *

When Fredd realized that some of the drugs they took were crystal meth, he didn't know what to do with it right away. He called one of his white boys, who lived in a small town outside of Philly named Wilkes-Barre.

Josh knew a lot about meth because he used to sell, use, cook, and distribute it. He told Fredd to meet him at his crib in an hour and they would discuss it then.

Fredd started heading in that direction so he could get back before Worlds came through. They were going to the club that night to celebrate their success in the game.

He parked in front of Josh's crib just as Josh was parking. They greeted one another and then headed inside.

"So show me what you got!" Josh stated, looking down at the gym bag that Fredd was carrying.

Fredd passed Josh the bag, and Josh set it on the table. When he opened it, he knew what it was just by looking at it. He motioned for Fredd to take a seat so he could explain everything and put him up on game.

"A lot of people don't make meth the right way. See, after they do the whole process with the lithium, cold pack, sulfuric acid, Sudafed, etc., they skip an entire process. Really, all they are making is bathtub crank, and then they wash it down with acetone and call it ice. Fucking lame! They have a couple of people tweaking because of that shit. Real ice like you just showed me right there is easy to come by if you know the right people. I know people who will take that off your hands ASAP if you're trying to sell it wholesale," Josh said.

"I'm still trying to figure out what I'm going to do with it," Fredd replied.

All kinds of thoughts were going through his head now. He wanted that fast money.

"Well, if you don't want to sell it like that, you can do it this way and still come up. Break it down to quarters, but instead of the .25, make them .18 so you'll have six quarters instead of four. Sell each one at $50, so that's $300 a gram at 1,000 grams. I think you can figure that out!" He smirked. Fredd was doing the numbers in his head while listening. "So as you can see, there's a lot you can do!"

"I don't want to hold it too long, so just see if you can get rid of it for a good price, and I'll break you off. I'm gonna leave it here with you, but don't try and play me," Fredd warned him.

"You know I'm not like that!"

"I'm just saying. Anyway, I have to go get ready 'cause me and my homie are hitting the club tonight. Just hit my cell when you're ready for me."

They shook hands, and Fredd left. He was about to make a hefty profit off of somebody else's work. He still had to split it with Zy and them, but it was all free money, so he didn't care.

BOOKS BY GOOD2GO AUTHORS

GOOD 2 GO FILMS PRESENTS

**THE HAND I WAS DEALT- FREE WEB SERIES
NOW AVAILABLE ON YOUTUBE!
YOUTUBE.COM/SILKWHITE212**

SEASON TWO NOW AVAILABLE

To order books, please fill out the order form below:

To order films please go to www.good2gofilms.com

Name:_____

Address:_____

City: _____ State: _____ Zip Code: _____

Phone:_____

Email:_____

Method of Payment: Check   VISA   MASTERCARD

Credit Card#:_____

Name as it appears on card: _____

Signature: _____

Item Name	Price	Qty	Amount
48 Hours to Die – Silk White	$14.99		
A Hustler's Dream - Ernest Morris	$14.99		
A Hustler's Dream 2 - Ernest Morris	$14.99		
Business Is Business – Silk White	$14.99		
Business Is Business 2 – Silk White	$14.99		
Business Is Business 3 – Silk White	$14.99		
Childhood Sweethearts – Jacob Spears	$14.99		
Childhood Sweethearts 2 – Jacob Spears	$14.99		
Childhood Sweethearts 3 - Jacob Spears	$14.99		
Childhood Sweethearts 4 - Jacob Spears	$14.99		
Flipping Numbers – Ernest Morris	$14.99		
Flipping Numbers 2 – Ernest Morris	$14.99		
He Loves Me, He Loves You Not - Mychea	$14.99		
He Loves Me, He Loves You Not 2 - Mychea	$14.99		
He Loves Me, He Loves You Not 3 - Mychea	$14.99		
He Loves Me, He Loves You Not 4 – Mychea	$14.99		
He Loves Me, He Loves You Not 5 – Mychea	$14.99		
Lost and Turned Out – Ernest Morris	$14.99		
Married To Da Streets – Silk White	$14.99		
M.E.R.C. - Make Every Rep Count Health and Fitness	$14.99		
My Besties – Asia Hill	$14.99		
My Besties 2 – Asia Hill	$14.99		
My Besties 3 – Asia Hill	$14.99		
My Besties 4 – Asia Hill	$14.99		
My Boyfriend's Wife - Mychea	$14.99		
My Boyfriend's Wife 2 – Mychea	$14.99		
Naughty Housewives – Ernest Morris	$14.99		
Naughty Housewives 2 – Ernest Morris	$14.99		
Never Be The Same – Silk White	$14.99		
Stranded – Silk White	$14.99		
Slumped – Jason Brent	$14.99		

Tears of a Hustler - Silk White	$14.99		
Tears of a Hustler 2 - Silk White	$14.99		
Tears of a Hustler 3 - Silk White	$14.99		
Tears of a Hustler 4- Silk White	$14.99		
Tears of a Hustler 5 – Silk White	$14.99		
Tears of a Hustler 6 – Silk White	$14.99		
The Panty Ripper - Reality Way	$14.99		
The Panty Ripper 3 – Reality Way	$14.99		
The Teflon Queen – Silk White	$14.99		
The Teflon Queen 2 – Silk White	$14.99		
The Teflon Queen 3 – Silk White	$14.99		
The Teflon Queen 4 – Silk White	$14.99		
The Teflon Queen 5 – Silk White	$14.99		
The Teflon Queen 6 - Silk White	$14.99		
The Vacation – Silk White	$14.99		
Tied To A Boss - J.L. Rose	$14.99		
Tied To A Boss 2 - J.L. Rose	$14.99		
Tied To A Boss 3 - J.L. Rose	$14.99		
Time Is Money - Silk White	$14.99		
Two Mask One Heart – Jacob Spears and Trayvon Jackson	$14.99		
Two Mask One Heart 2 – Jacob Spears and Trayvon Jackson	$14.99		
Two Mask One Heart 3 – Jacob Spears and Trayvon Jackson	$14.99		
Young Goonz – Reality Way	$14.99		
Young Legend – J.L. Rose	$14.99		
Subtotal:			
Tax:			
Shipping (Free) U.S. Media Mail:			
Total:			

Make Checks Payable To:
Good2Go Publishing
7311 W Glass Lane,
Laveen, AZ 85339